W9-AZQ-022

Neveah stole a sidelong glance at Xavier. Before she could stop to question the sudden impulse, she leaned over to kiss his cheek.

Unfortunately, he turned his head at the same time.

In that exhilarating instant, a rush of pleasure swept through her, torching her blood. As their eyes locked, every instinct screamed at Neveah to pull back before it was too late. But then Xavier angled his head slightly, molding his mouth to hers. And she closed her eyes, surrendering with a low moan.

His lips were even softer than she'd remembered, lush and unbelievably sensual. His hand came up, cupping the curve of her cheek as he deepened the kiss. He tasted like cotton candy and masculinity, sweet and decadently sinful. She quivered as he traced his tongue over her lips and licked the soft inner flesh, coaxing her to open for him.

His tongue captured hers, tasting and stroking her until she thought she would go up in flames. He whispered her name—an endearment, a prayer, a call to seduction. Her body strained against his, shamelessly heeding the summons.

"Well, well, well. So *this* is where you've been hiding."

Books by Maureen Smith

Kimani Romance

A Legal Affair
A Guilty Affair
A Risky Affair
Secret Agent Seduction
Touch of Heaven
Recipe for Temptation
Tempt Me at Midnight
Imagine Us

Kimani Arabesque

With Every Breath
A Heartbeat Away

MAUREEN SMITH

is the author of seventeen novels and one novella. She received a B.A. in English from the University of Maryland, with a minor in creative writing. She is a former freelance writer whose articles were featured in various print and online publications. Since the release of her debut novel in 2002, Maureen has been nominated for three *RT Book Reviews* Reviewers' Choice Awards and fourteen Emma Awards, and has won the Romance in Color Reviewers' Choice Awards for New Author of the Year and Romantic Suspense of the Year. Her novel *Secret Agent Seduction* won the 2010 Emma Award for Best Romantic Suspense.

Maureen lives in San Antonio, Texas, with her husband, two children and a miniature schnauzer. She loves to hear from readers and can be reached at author@maureen-smith.com. Please visit her website at www.maureen-smith.com for news about her upcoming releases.

Imagine US

MAUREEN SMITH

KIMANI
ROMANCE

If you purchased this book without a cover you should be aware
that this book is stolen property. It was reported as "unsold and
destroyed" to the publisher, and neither the author nor the
publisher has received any payment for this "stripped book."

To every reader who asked for more Maynes.

 KIMANI PRESS™

Recycling programs
for this product may
not exist in your area.

ISBN-13: 978-0-373-86211-5

IMAGINE US

Copyright © 2011 by Maureen Smith

All rights reserved. The reproduction, transmission or utilization
of this work in whole or in part in any form by any electronic, mechanical
or other means, now known or hereafter invented, including xerography,
photocopying and recording, or in any information storage or retrieval
system, is forbidden without written permission. For permission please
contact Kimani Press, Editorial Office, 233 Broadway, New York, NY
10279 U.S.A.

This is a work of fiction. Names, characters, places and incidents are
either the product of the author's imagination or are used fictitiously,
and any resemblance to actual persons, living or dead, business establishments,
events or locales is entirely coincidental.

® and TM are trademarks. Trademarks indicated with ® are registered in
the United States Patent and Trademark Office, the Canadian Trade Marks
Office and/or other countries.

www.kimanipress.com

Printed in U.S.A.

Dear Reader,

In 2009 you were introduced to the Mayne family in my novel *Touch of Heaven*. I was so pleased to receive so many emails from readers asking to see more of Warrick's siblings that I decided to create the Mayne Attraction series. And next in the lineup is Xavier Mayne, who's on a mission to win back the one and only woman he has ever loved.

It was hard for me to keep high school sweethearts Xavier and Neveah apart for thirteen whole years. But I hope you will enjoy the emotional, romantic journey that brings them back together again. Absence definitely makes the heart grow fonder.

As always, please share your thoughts with me at author@maureen-smith.com. You can even tell me which sibling's story you'd like to read next. I always welcome feedback.

Until next time, happy reading!

Maureen Smith

Chapter 1

"I feel like a voyeur."

The woman's hushed confession drew a chuckle from her companion, a silver-haired gentleman clad in a black tuxedo. The handsome couple stood before a canvas oil painting mounted on a wall. The portrait captured a nude man and woman locked in a torrid embrace, their sensuously entwined bodies framed against a scorching sunset.

"Perhaps that was her intention," the tuxedoed man postulated. "To make us feel like voyeurs, as though we were intruding upon an intimate encounter between two lovers."

"Perhaps," the woman agreed. "At any rate, it's absolutely mesmerizing. Such passion, such raw sensuality conveyed in each brushstroke. It's definitely her most risqué work to date."

Neveah Symon hid a private smile as she stood beside the two art collectors appraising her latest work.

"I wonder what inspired this particular piece," the woman mused.

Lifting her champagne flute to her lips, Neveah offered, "Maybe she was thinking about how long it had been since she'd gotten laid."

With a scandalized gasp, the woman turned to gape at her. "I beg your par—"

"*There* you are! I've been looking all over for you."

The newcomer's voice belonged to a tall, beautiful woman with a butterscotch complexion and a sylphlike figure. Neveah had only a glimpse of Jordan Harper's tight-lipped smile before she grabbed Neveah's arm and hastily ushered her away from the frowning couple.

"I can't let you out of my sight for one damn minute," Jordan muttered, shaking her head in exasperation as she led Neveah through a crowd of people eating canapés, sipping champagne and socializing. "You just don't know how to behave yourself."

Neveah laughed. "I was mingling with our guests. What's wrong with that?"

Jordan snorted. "We both know you weren't *mingling*. You were making mischief."

"Mischief? What are you talking about?"

Jordan shot her a knowing look. "I overheard what you told that couple."

"So what?" Neveah grinned unabashedly. "Maybe I *was* horny when I painted *Golden Ecstasy*. Contrary to popular belief, not everything I create is inspired by angst or tragedy. Sometimes all it takes is good old-fashioned lust to get my juices flowing. Pun definitely intended," she added with a wicked chuckle.

Jordan shook her head, lips quirking as she fought back a smile. "Be that as it may," she said, steering Neveah into an empty corner, "I'd appreciate it if you kept that, ah, revelation to yourself. There's nothing deep or philosophical about being creatively inspired by lust—"

Neveah laughed. "I beg to differ."

Jordan was not only Neveah's best friend of sixteen years, she was also her business partner. The art gallery owned by the two women was situated in a converted warehouse that featured high ceilings, pristine white walls, gleaming hardwood floors and recessed lighting. It was located in Houston's theater district, which was home to an eclectic community of thespians, artists and musicians. Although the gallery had showcased the works of several world-renowned painters and sculptors over the years, it was—first and foremost—a venue for local and emerging artists to gain exposure. For that reason, Neveah had insisted on limiting the number of her pieces to be sold tonight.

"Do you have any idea who that couple was?" Jordan demanded.

Neveah sipped her champagne, idly surveying the crowd of elegantly dressed strangers milling around. "What couple?"

"The couple you were scandalizing before I intervened. Do you know who they were? None other than Eugene and Margot Rosenblum."

Neveah looked blank. "Who?"

Jordan eyed her incredulously. "Don't tell me you've never heard of them before! They only happen to be two of the most prominent art critics in the country. They've reviewed your work in *The New York Times* and *The New Yorker*—"

Neveah grinned. "Favorably, I hope?"

"Of course. They *love* your work. And since they're both native Texans, they're especially partial to anything you do. They're going to enjoy meeting you at the charity auction. Which brings me to my next point. No one's supposed to know that you're back in the States, remember? You're supposed to make your grand appearance in two weeks. If Seth knew that you were here tonight, he'd kill *both* of us."

Neveah chuckled at the mention of her longtime manager,

who scheduled all her publicity appearances and handled her business affairs so she could immerse herself in her art. A consummate professional, Seth Daniels had been a godsend to her, even if he *was* high-strung.

"That's why I didn't want you to attend tonight's showing," Jordan fussed. "I knew you wouldn't be able to keep a low profile. What if the Rosenblums had recognized you?"

Neveah chuckled. "Relax. No one's going to recognize me."

"How do you know?"

"For starters, I've been living overseas for the past thirteen years and I rarely do interviews, which means I haven't been photographed very often. Besides, someone would have to be looking *real* hard to recognize me under this thing—" she touched the edge of the wide-brimmed black hat that slanted over her eyes "—you forced me to wear."

"That *thing*," Jordan said archly, "is a Kokin original. And what are you complaining about? You look fabulous. Like a bona fide fashionista."

"That's me, all right," Neveah quipped sardonically. "Fashionista extraordinaire."

Jordan laughed, acknowledging the absurdity of the remark. Neveah was the furthest thing from a "fashionista" you could ever find. With her trademark peasant blouses, colorful dashikis and gypsy skirts, she was the epitome of the free-spirited bohemian who was unconcerned with the latest fashion trends. So it was no wonder that she felt out of sorts in the slinky black dress and strappy high heels she'd reluctantly agreed to wear for that evening's reception.

"Seriously though, Neveah." Jordan's tone had gentled. "You *do* look wonderful, and not just because you're wearing an outfit I handpicked for you. You're a sight for sore eyes. I've missed you, and I'm really glad you're home."

"Oh, Jordy." Neveah smiled softly, touched by her best

friend's heartfelt words. "I've missed you, too. And I can't tell you enough how grateful I am for everything you've done with the gallery. *None* of this—" she gestured to encompass the large, buzzing crowd "—would have been possible without your dedication and hard work."

"Oh, hush." Jordan waved off Neveah's gratitude, her cheeks pinkening with embarrassment. "I haven't done anything you wouldn't have done if you'd been living here. And let's not forget that without your vision and financial backing, there'd *be* no gallery."

Neveah grinned. "You just can't do it, can you?"

"What?"

"You just can't accept a simple thank-you."

Jordan chuckled, draping an arm around Neveah's shoulders. "Don't worry. Now that you're back home, I'll be putting you to work. And trust me, by the end of the week, thanking me will be the *last* thing you want to do."

Both women laughed.

"Oh, look, there's Nicolás Garcia." Jordan smiled and waved at someone across the room.

"Another art critic?" Neveah asked.

"No, he's a board member of the Houston Arts Alliance. I'd love to introduce you to him, but I'd better not. If he goes back and tells anyone that he met you tonight, word will get around, and Seth will kick my ass. I'll introduce you to Nicolás at the charity auction in two weeks."

"Okay," Neveah agreed, "but he's making his way over here to greet you, so you'd better head him off."

"Good idea." Jordan leveled one last warning glance at Neveah. "Behave."

Neveah grinned. "Yes, ma'am."

After Jordan departed, Neveah's gaze was drawn to an abstract painting displayed on a nearby wall. The piece had been done by a local artist named Topaz. Jordan had been raving about his work for months, and Neveah could understand why. His impressive staining technique and use of unusual color combinations demonstrated an aptitude rarely possessed by beginning artists. Neveah looked forward to meeting him. That is, once her manager allowed her to officially emerge from hiding.

"Neveah."

She turned at the sound of her name. And nearly dropped her empty champagne glass.

The man who'd addressed her was so handsome he took her breath away. His skin was the richly decadent color of caramel. His face was a mesmerizing study in contrasts—the masculinity of heavy eyebrows, granite cheekbones and a square jaw juxtaposed by thick, curly eyelashes and a lush, sensual mouth framed by a trim goatee. His eyes were heavy lidded, and as dark and sinful as melted chocolate. He was tall, with broad shoulders, long legs and a powerful frame that was wonderfully accentuated by the cut of his expensive black suit.

As Neveah stared at him, the room began to spin. She swallowed hard and fought to keep her balance, which was a feat considering that she'd just received the biggest shock of her life, coming face to face with the man who'd broken her heart and shattered her dreams thirteen years ago.

Xavier Mayne gazed down at her with deep-set eyes that traced her features beneath the low brim of her hat. She wanted to duck her head, turn away from him. But she couldn't. As her heart drummed wildly, she could only stare at him and wonder what he was doing there. Surely he knew that he was the absolute *last* person on earth she wanted to see.

"I can't believe you're here." His voice was deep, dark and dangerously intoxicating. "It's been a long time."

Not long enough, Neveah wanted to say, but her vocal chords had apparently gone on strike. She couldn't believe that the gorgeous, Versace-clad stranger who stood before her was the same roughneck who'd stolen her heart—along with her virginity—a lifetime ago. His face was leaner, tougher, the angular contours more sharply defined. His silky black hair was cut close to his scalp in lieu of the cornrows he'd once favored. Also gone were the diamond stud earring, the iced-out chain and the platinum three-finger "Rated XXX" ring he'd famously sported. But it wasn't just the absence of bling that intrigued Neveah. The grown-up version of Xavier exuded confidence, finesse and a smoldering masculinity that completely robbed her of speech.

After a prolonged silence, Xavier's expression softened with concern. "Are you all right?"

Absolutely not!

"I'm fine." Her voice barely rose above a whisper. "What are you doing here?"

"I came to see you."

Neveah shivered, her fingers reflexively tightening around the stem of her glass. "How did you know I was back in town?"

"Does it matter?"

"It does to me."

"Why?" He moved closer, close enough to breach her personal space and set her pulse hammering. She dragged in a shaky breath, then wished she hadn't as the subtle, spicy notes of his cologne invaded her senses. Even after all the years she'd spent trying to purge him from her system, his presence still wreaked pure, unadulterated havoc on her body.

Heat gathered beneath her skin as his penetrating gaze roamed the length of her before slowly returning to her face. "You look amazing, Neveah," he said huskily.

She hated the way her heartbeat quickened, hated that she still loved the way her name rolled off his tongue like a lover's caress.

She swallowed with difficulty. "You shouldn't have come here."

"Did you really think I would stay away?"

"I *hoped* you would."

"I couldn't," he said simply.

They stared at each other.

When Neveah recently made the momentous decision to return home to Houston, she'd known there was a strong chance that she would run into her old flame. But she hadn't expected it to happen this soon. And she certainly hadn't expected *him* to seek her out after all these years.

"I've missed you, Neveah," he said softly. "I'm glad you came back home. You belong here."

Anger flared inside her chest. "I didn't come back for you. In fact, I don't want—"

"More wine, miss?" interrupted a white-gloved waiter carrying a silver tray.

Grateful for the distraction, Neveah blurted, "Yes. Please."

After refilling Neveah's champagne glass, the waiter looked to Xavier, who politely declined.

Once the man had moved off, Neveah took a long sip of her drink, hoping the chilled wine would help calm her frayed nerves.

Dipping his hands into his pants pockets, Xavier watched her with a faintly amused expression.

"What?" she snapped.

"There was a time you could barely handle *one* glass of wine, let alone two. After one drink, it was pretty much lights-out for you."

Neveah smirked. "Yeah, well, I've done a lot of growing up since then. What about you? Still knocking back forties and getting drunk with your friends?"

"Not quite." A small, self-deprecating smile touched his mouth. "I do my drinking alone these days."

Neveah faltered for a moment, disarmed by the trace of sorrow in his voice. She couldn't imagine Xavier Mayne doing *anything* alone. In all the years she'd known him, he had never lacked for companionship—especially of the female variety. Which was why their relationship had been doomed from the start.

As the painful memories threatened to surface, Neveah took a step backward, wishing that she and Xavier were once again separated by thousands of miles, although no amount of distance could ever completely cure her of him.

"I have to go," she announced.

"This early?"

"Yes. I wasn't even supposed to be here tonight."

"I'm glad you were," he murmured.

She didn't know how to respond to that. So she didn't. "Well, it was…nice to see you again. Take care."

She should have known it wouldn't be that easy.

As she moved to make her escape, Xavier stopped her cold in her tracks by saying, "I need you, Neveah."

Chapter 2

Neveah stared at him, heart knocking against her ribs. "What did you just say?"

Xavier held her stunned gaze. "I have a proposition for you."

Her mouth went dry, even as she instantly rationalized that he couldn't *possibly* be referring to anything sexual. Striving for composure, she said, "Sorry. I'm not interested."

"Why don't you hear me out before you turn me down?" he drawled, humor threading his deep voice.

Like a lit fuse, her temper flared. "I don't need to hear you out," she snapped. "I have no interest in anything you—"

At that moment another couple wandered over to admire Topaz's painting, their presence reminding Neveah that she and Xavier were not alone. The last thing she wanted was to cause a scene at her own art gallery. Jordan would never forgive her, and when word got back to Seth, he would have an apoplectic seizure.

As though he'd intercepted her thoughts, Xavier glanced

around the crowded room and suggested, "Maybe we should find somewhere to talk in private."

"That won't be necessary," Neveah said as they moved away from the other couple. "We have nothing more to say to each other, Xavier."

He stopped and turned to face her, forcing her to meet his dark, probing gaze. "It's been thirteen years, Neveah," he said quietly. "How long are you going to keep punishing me for what happened in the past?"

A wave of white-hot fury blazed through her. "How *dare* you?" she hissed in a harsh whisper. "What the hell gives you the right to waltz back into my life after all these years and make demands of me? I don't owe you a *damn* thing, least of all an explanation for my actions. As you just pointed out, it's been thirteen years. *I've* moved on with my life. I suggest you do the same!"

"I can't." He gave her a knowing look. "And, apparently, neither can you."

Choking with outrage—and unable to deny what he'd said—Neveah was just seconds away from throwing her champagne in his face when a sugary feminine voice intruded. "Oh my God! Is that who I *think* it is?"

Neveah and Xavier turned to watch the approach of a voluptuous, honey-toned woman wearing a skimpy red cocktail dress and matching stilettos. Neveah guessed right away that the newcomer was not one of *her* adoring fans, but rather, Xavier's.

Beaming with delight, the young woman launched herself at Xavier, arms looping around his neck, large breasts crushed against his chest. "I *thought* that was you!" she squealed excitedly, turning the heads of several people nearby.

Neveah's insides twisted as Xavier chuckled, briefly returning the woman's embrace before drawing back to smile at her. "It's good to see you again, Alyson. How have you been?"

"Wonderful." She sighed. "I just got back from Paris. My parents rewarded me with the trip for earning my master's degree."

"That's great news," Xavier said warmly. "Congratulations."

"Thank you, Xavier," she gushed, smiling radiantly. "It took me a little longer than I would have preferred, but good things come to those who wait, right?"

"Absolutely." Xavier smiled lazily before turning to Neveah at his side and performing the introductions. "Alyson, I'd like you to meet Neveah Symon. Neveah, this is Alyson Kelley."

As the two women exchanged cordial greetings, Alyson looked Neveah over with a cool, calculating gleam in her eyes, openly sizing her up. Neveah couldn't help returning the appraisal, estimating that the other woman couldn't be more than twenty-five, tops.

"You wouldn't happen to be *the* Neveah Symon, would you?"

Neveah smiled wryly. "Last I checked."

"Wow." Alyson shot a reproving glance at Xavier. "You never told me you were friends with a famous painter."

"My apologies," Xavier murmured, meeting Neveah's gaze. "I'm sure if we'd ever discussed art, it would have come up eventually."

Alyson laughed, sliding him an intimate look that left little doubt in Neveah's mind that they'd probably done more screwing than talking during the course of their relationship.

Unnerved by the thought, she plastered on a bright smile and inquired casually, "How did you two meet?"

Alyson beamed. "We met five years ago when I was

crowned Miss Houston. Xavier was one of the pageant judges."

He dated a beauty queen? Neveah thought in exasperated disgust. That was just *too* predictable, even for a notorious womanizer like Xavier.

"We didn't become involved until *after* I'd won the title." Alyson smiled coyly at Xavier, whose dark gaze had never wavered from Neveah's. "He didn't want to be accused of having a conflict of interest. It was very important to him to protect his precious community center from scandal, which I totally admired and respected. However, I'm not ashamed to admit that I pursued him until I wore him down."

Neveah smiled narrowly at Xavier. "I'm sure *that* didn't take very long."

Alyson laughed, completely missing the way Xavier's jaw clenched. "It took long enough. But like I said before, good things come to those who wait."

"Congratulations." Neveah sipped her champagne, wishing she had something stronger. *Much* stronger.

"So, Neveah, how long have you been back in Houston?" Alyson asked curiously. "I thought I read somewhere that you were enjoying the life of a recluse in Senegal. What brings you back home?"

Bristling at the intrusiveness of the question, Neveah murmured, "I came back for personal reasons."

Alyson didn't take the hint. "Are you planning to stay permanently?" she prodded, no doubt wondering whether Neveah intended to compete for Xavier's affections.

Before Neveah could respond, Xavier interjected humorously, "Damn, baby girl, did you just graduate from law school or something? Ease up on the cross-examination."

"I'm sorry," Alyson mumbled, reminding Neveah of a spoiled child who'd just been scolded.

"Oh, that's quite all right." Neveah smiled sweetly. "Let me assure you, Alyson, that you have nothing to worry about. He's *all* yours." As Xavier's expression darkened with annoyance, she nodded curtly to both of them. "Enjoy the rest of your evening."

With that, she spun on her heel and strode away.

After downing the rest of her champagne, she placed her empty glass on the tray of a passing waiter and headed from the main gallery. As she weaved through the sea of milling guests, she was grateful for the anonymity she'd enjoyed throughout the evening. She was in no frame of mind to interact with her fans or sign autographs.

She was still seething with fury when she reached the closed door to Jordan's office, which was located at the rear of the building. Neveah twisted the knob and marched into the room—and stopped short at the sight of Jordan passionately entwined with a young, attractive man sporting shoulder-length dreadlocks.

Hearing Neveah's shocked gasp, the couple sprang apart. Jordan hopped off the desk, hastily yanking down her dress.

"I—I'm sorry," Neveah stammered awkwardly. "I didn't know you were in here. I just came to get my purse. I'll come back—"

"No, wait! You don't have to go." Jordan looked flustered. "We were just, um…that is, we were—"

The man was staring at Neveah in shocked recognition. "Are you Neveah Symon?"

"I am." She smiled. "And you are…?"

"Shemar Reeves. But I go by Topaz."

"*You're* Topaz?" Neveah cast a surprised glance at Jordan, who blushed and dropped her gaze.

Shemar—Topaz—swiftly crossed the room to shake Neveah's hand. "It's such an honor to meet you. I've been a huge fan of your work for years."

That was saying a lot, considering he didn't look a day over twenty with his baby-smooth skin and boyish smile.

"I've been admiring your work, as well," Neveah told him. "You're very talented."

He beamed with pleasure. "That means a lot to me, coming from you."

Jordan discreetly cleared her throat. "Topaz, why don't you, ah, head back to the reception? I'll rejoin you shortly."

"Okay." He winked at her. "I'll be waiting."

As soon as he'd departed, Neveah closed the door and rounded on her best friend. "Jordan Kate Harper, you got some 'splainin' to do!"

"I know, I know." Jordan groaned, clapping both hands to her flushed cheeks as she sank into the chair behind her desk.

Neveah advanced on her. "I can't believe you! After the way you lectured *me* about misbehaving tonight, I walk in here and catch you practically in flagrante delicto with one of our exhibiting artists!"

"I know! It's crazy. I don't know what the hell came over me."

"Oh, *I've* got a pretty good idea," Neveah said with a knowing grin. "Shall I spell it out for you? *L-U-S-T.*"

Again Jordan groaned, turning several shades redder.

Neveah laughed, her own troubles momentarily forgotten as she claimed the visitor chair opposite Jordan's desk. "Girl, why didn't you tell me you and Topaz were dating?"

"We're not!"

"Oh?" Neveah arched a brow. "So what I just witnessed—"

"—was a one-time thing!" At Neveah's skeptical look, Jordan hastened to elaborate. "I told him that I had some contracts he needed to sign, so he followed me back here to the office. I should have known something was up when he closed the door behind him. He told me that he's been attracted to me ever since we met. The next thing I knew, he was kissing me!"

Neveah grinned slyly. "You didn't appear to mind very much."

Jordan shrugged, grinning sheepishly. "What can I say? The man is one helluva kisser."

"You shameless hussy! That 'man' looks all of twenty years old!"

"He's twenty-four."

"So he's ten years younger than you."

Jordan glared at her. "I can do the math."

Neveah laughed, holding up her hands. "I'm just sayin'."

"Yeah, I know what you're saying. I've become a cougar." Jordan heaved a disgusted sigh, shaking her head at the ceiling. "Lord, why is it that the first guy I've been interested in since the breakup has to be totally wrong for me?"

The "breakup" she was referring to was the painful split with her longtime boyfriend, whose confessed preference for men had left Jordan reeling with shock, anger and confusion. She'd taken refuge at Neveah's beachside cottage in Senegal, where she'd been fed, held and nurtured through her heartbreak.

"So you *are* interested in Topaz," Neveah said.

Jordan hesitated, then nodded reluctantly. "I've been attracted to him from the very beginning. Not only is he sexy as hell, but he's also incredibly talented, smart and worldly. I mean, we can talk about anything and everything. Sometimes I wonder if *I'm* deep enough for *him*," she admitted with a wry chuckle. "You know how you artists *feel* things on a more emotional level than the rest of us."

Neveah smiled softly. "If what you say about him is true, then he doesn't sound so wrong for you after all."

Jordan shrugged. "Maybe. Still want your purse?"

"Yes, please."

Reaching inside her desk drawer, Jordan removed Neveah's black satin clutch and passed it to her. "So you're leaving, huh? What finally convinced you to heed my advice?"

"*Who,* you mean," Neveah muttered darkly.

"What are you talking about?"

Neveah hesitated, then inhaled a deep breath and let it out slowly. "Xavier is here."

Jordan's eyes widened. "*Xavier?* Are you serious?"

Neveah's mouth twisted into a grim smile. "Believe me, this isn't something I would joke about."

"No," Jordan quietly agreed, "you wouldn't."

She knew better than anyone how utterly devastated Neveah had been when she and Xavier broke up. She also knew the terrible secret Neveah had harbored for the past thirteen years, a secret that had nearly destroyed her.

Jordan's expression gentled. "Are you okay?"

Neveah nodded, swallowing tightly.

"Did he…come alone?"

"I think so." Neveah laughed bitterly. "But he probably won't *leave* alone."

"What do you mean?"

"While we were talking, we were joined by one of his exes. A former beauty queen with big, perky breasts and a sex-kitten laugh. When I left them, she had her claws sunk pretty deep."

"Ahhh." Jordan nodded knowingly. "So you've met the lovely Alyson Kelley."

Neveah rolled her eyes. "Unfortunately."

"Well, if it's any consolation to you, their affair didn't last very long. According to the rumor mill, Alyson was caught up with traveling and becoming the next Miss Texas—which didn't happen, by the way—and Xavier was consumed with establishing the community center he'd founded with his brothers. So their romance fizzled out pretty quickly."

"Well," Neveah muttered sourly, "it's pretty obvious that Alyson wants to rekindle their relationship. She all but told me to go back to Africa so she'd have Xavier all to herself."

Jordan snorted. "She should know better than that. No woman's *ever* had that man all to herself."

"Yeah," Neveah agreed sadly, "don't I know it?"

Belatedly realizing her gaffe, Jordan shook her head at the ceiling and muttered, "Open mouth. Insert foot."

Neveah chuckled grimly. "It's okay. You were just speaking the truth. I'm a big girl—I can take it."

Jordan frowned. "I wonder how he found out you'd be here tonight."

"He wouldn't tell me. Anyway, it doesn't mat—"

She was interrupted by a knock at the door. "Hey, Jordan," called their young assistant, Chelsea. "Is Neveah in there with you?"

"Yeeeaaah," Jordan answered, drawing out the word cautiously. "Why do you ask?"

"There's a man out here looking for her. He must have seen my name tag and figured out that I work here, 'cause he stopped me and asked me to track down Neveah for him."

Neveah and Jordan traded sharp glances.

Xavier, they mouthed simultaneously.

A split second later, Neveah was out of her chair and hooking the jeweled strap of her purse over her shoulder. "Stall him," she whispered to Jordan, who nodded quickly.

"Tell him she'll be out in a minute!" she instructed Chelsea.

"Okeydokey." The girl paused, her next words laced with naughty mischief. "By the way, did I mention what a drop-dead-gorgeous hottie he is? *Meeoow!*"

Jordan laughed, then clapped a hand over her mouth as Neveah shot her a dirty look.

"Et tu, Brute?" she said through gritted teeth.

"Sorry." Jordan grinned sheepishly. "He *is* a hottie, though. Always was."

With an exasperated shake of her head, Neveah strode across the room and hurriedly slipped out the back door that led to the rear parking lot. As she sped away from the gallery minutes later, she wished she could congratulate herself for making a clean getaway.

But she knew she hadn't seen the last of Xavier. For some unfathomable reason, he seemed hell-bent on bulldozing his way back into her life—as if he hadn't caused enough carnage the first time around.

Neveah would have to be the world's biggest fool to give him another chance to hurt her.

Fortunately for her, her mama didn't raise no fool.

Chapter 3

Xavier paced up and down the small foyer located at the rear of the building. A security guard manned the entrance to a corridor that presumably led to the art gallery's business offices. Between directing guests to the restrooms and flipping through his newspaper, the man kept one eye trained on Xavier, silently daring him to make one false move.

Xavier chuckled darkly to himself.

Several years ago, he would have challenged the security guard's authority by muscling him aside and charging down the corridor in search of Neveah. And he wouldn't have apologized for his boorish behavior, because back then he'd been a brash, hot-tempered brawler with a huge chip on his shoulder and the emotional maturity of an adolescent.

But things were different now. He was trying to be a better man. Trying to be the kind of man Neveah had always wanted—and deserved.

The click of high heels on polished hardwood brought his head up. As soon as he saw Jordan walking toward him, he knew he'd been given the slip. And he swore under his breath, cursing his stupidity for not anticipating that Neveah would cut and run.

Just as she'd done thirteen years ago, turning his world upside down.

As Jordan approached, Xavier watched her with a surly expression. "Where's Neveah?"

"It's nice to see you, too," Jordan said drily. "It's been a while, hasn't it? I think the last time we ran into each other was at the mayor's birthday celebration last year. I heard you've recently been appointed to serve on her community revitalization task force—"

"Where's Neveah?" Xavier cut her off.

"She left." Jordan paused. "And I think you know why."

His chest tightened. He regarded Jordan for another moment, then nodded curtly, pivoted on his heel and stalked off.

"She doesn't want to see you, Xavier," Jordan called after him. "You had to know that when you showed up here tonight. You had to know you'd only upset her. But, as usual, you put your own selfish needs above hers."

Xavier stopped midstride, then turned to meet her accusing gaze. "*I'm* selfish?"

Panic flickered across her face as he slowly, deliberately, retraced his steps to where she stood.

"Tell me something, Jordan," he drawled, stopping directly in front of her. "Does Neveah know about that night?"

Jordan eyed him warily. "What night?"

"Come now," he mocked. "Are you telling me that you don't remember the night you came on to me?"

As the blood slowly leached out of her face, he smiled narrowly. "Ahhh. It's all coming back to you now, isn't it?"

She gulped visibly. "Xavier—"

"No?" he taunted ruthlessly. "Details still a little fuzzy?

Here, let me refresh your memory. About thirteen years ago, you and Neveah attended a party at my apartment. Since the party ended so late, and you'd both had one too many drinks, I didn't want you getting on the road and driving all the way back to school in Austin. So I told you guys to crash at my place and head out in the morning. Sometime in the middle of the night, while I was sound asleep on the sofa, someone tiptoed into the living room and climbed on top of me. But it wasn't my girlfriend. No, *she* was knocked out in my bedroom, blissfully oblivious to the fact that her best friend was trying to screw her man. Fortunately, *he* had the good sense to tell the little backstabber to take her silly ass back to bed before he threw her out of his damn apartment." Xavier paused, lips twisted mockingly as he looked at Jordan. "Any of this ringing a bell yet?"

Her face had turned crimson. "You bastard," she hissed. "I was *drunk* that night!"

"Maybe you were," he murmured. "And maybe you weren't."

Her nostrils flared, her lips pressed so tightly together the skin blanched. Dropping her guilty gaze, she mumbled, "I wasn't myself that night. Don't forget I'd had a horrible argument with my boyfriend earlier that day. I was feeling lonely and vulnerable, and being around you and Neveah— watching how lovey-dovey you were with each other—didn't help. I know that doesn't excuse my behavior, and God knows I felt lower than a pile of shit after you sent me packing." Her eyes lifted to his, searching his hard face. "I tried to apologize to you and explain my actions the next day, but you didn't want to hear it. You thoroughly hated my guts and thought I was the worst friend in the world. But you never told Neveah what happened. I drove myself crazy waiting for the other shoe to drop. But you kept your silence. So why are you dredging it up now, after all these years. *Why,* for God's sake?"

"Oh, I don't know." Xavier smirked at her. "Maybe I think it's time for you to unburden yourself of this terrible secret once and for all."

Stricken, Jordan shook her head vigorously. "I can't tell her."

"Then maybe *I* should."

She stared at him, her eyes filled with dread. "You wouldn't dare."

She was right. He would never deliberately hurt Neveah by divulging the truth about her best friend's past betrayal. But right now he was angry and desperate enough to say anything.

"If you tell her about that night," Jordan blustered, "don't assume *you'll* walk away smelling like roses. She's going to be furious with you for keeping such a secret from her."

"Probably," Xavier conceded mildly. "But the difference between you and me is that I have nothing to lose. Neveah's been out of my life for a long time now. She couldn't possibly hate me any more than she already does. You, on the other hand, have everything to lose. Your best friend *and* your business partner, who—judging by the success of tonight's reception—has made you quite a wealthy woman over the years."

Tears brimmed in Jordan's eyes. "Not a day goes by that I don't regret coming on to you that night, Xavier. Believe me when I tell you that the last thing I ever wanted to do was hurt Neveah. I love her like my own sister."

"So I know how absolutely devastated you'd be if she severed you from her life, the way she did to me."

Swallowing tightly at the thought, Jordan dashed a tear from the corner of her eye. "You broke Neveah's heart," she grumbled. "If you think I'm going to start championing your cause just because you're trying to blackmail me, think again."

Xavier scowled. "I'm not asking you to champion my cause. I fully intend to win Neveah back, with or without your damn approval. And if I really wanted to blackmail you, I would have done so when Neveah first broke up with me. God knows I could have used an advocate back then. But I don't need you to convince your friend to give me a second chance. I'll do that on my own. Having said that, there *is* something you can do for me."

Jordan frowned, mutinously crossing her arms.

A tense silence lapsed between them.

Xavier impatiently waited it out.

He saw the grudging resignation in Jordan's eyes before she shook her head and heaved a deep sigh. "Tell me what you want."

After leaving the art gallery, Xavier was too restless to embark on the long drive home. So he took a detour and headed toward the Third Ward, arriving shortly at a sprawling redbrick facility that was located minutes away from the housing projects he and his family had once called home.

He smiled when he spotted his younger sister's Ford Fusion, the lone vehicle in the otherwise deserted parking lot. Since becoming a youth counselor at the community center, Yolanda Mayne could often be found working late into the evening, planning recreational activities and writing progress reports for the at-risk children under her supervision. Her radiant personality and untiring commitment to her young charges had made her the most popular counselor at the Shawn Mayne Community Center, named in honor of a beloved cousin who'd been killed in a drive-by shooting.

After letting himself into the locked building, Xavier bypassed the elevator and bounded up three flights of stairs to reach the third floor, which housed the center's administrative offices. Sure enough, light from Yolanda's office spilled into the corridor.

Reaching the open doorway, Xavier poked his head inside and grinned at the sight that greeted him. Yolanda sat behind a large desk littered with paperwork, file folders and textbooks. She was fast asleep, her head propped up on her palm and her lips parted as she snored softly.

Leaning one shoulder on the doorjamb, Xavier quietly studied his sister, knowing she wouldn't have tolerated such an inspection if she'd been awake. Unbeknownst to many who knew her, Yolanda had always been insecure about her appearance, although most women would probably kill for the flawless caramel complexion, camera-ready looks and long, lustrous black hair she'd been blessed with. She'd never believed she was pretty enough, or smart enough, or worthy enough—and those deep-seated insecurities had ultimately contributed to her downfall.

Watching her sleep, Xavier felt a surge of protective tenderness wash over him. Less than two years ago, Yolanda had been confined to a prison cell that was half the size of the office she now occupied. She'd been convicted as an accessory to armed robbery, a crime that had left an innocent man permanently paralyzed and had landed Yolanda behind bars for twelve years. Xavier and the rest of the family had been shocked and devastated by the outcome of the trial, and the years that followed had taken a severe emotional toll on everyone. Throughout her incarceration, Yolanda had staunchly maintained her innocence, claiming that she'd been wrongfully accused by her best friend, Raina, who'd testified in court against her. The family had sided with Yolanda, unwilling to accept the unthinkable alternative—that she *was* guilty. But shortly after her release from prison, Yolanda had assembled the family to make a stunning announcement. On the night of the robbery, she *had* accompanied her boyfriend to the convenience store where he'd confronted and shot the clerk who'd refused to open the cash register.

The entire family had been floored by Yolanda's confession, reacting to the news with outraged silence. Bursting into tears, Yolanda had expressed her deep sorrow and regret for the role she'd played in ruining an innocent man's life, maliciously slandering her best friend and betraying her family's love and trust. She'd humbly begged their forgiveness and vowed that she would spend the rest of her life atoning for her past sins.

When her criminal record hindered her employment search, Xavier had offered her a job at the community center. It turned out to be the smartest move he'd ever made. Mentoring abused and neglected youth gave Yolanda an opportunity to positively influence the children's lives and help steer them on the right path. She'd made it her personal mission to rescue as many as she could from making the same mistakes she had.

As she snorted softly in her sleep, Xavier grinned mischievously. Straightening from the doorway, he crept across the room and leaned down to bark in his sister's ear, "Sleeping on the job again?"

Yolanda jerked violently awake.

As Xavier burst out laughing, she stared up at him in dazed confusion, which quickly gave way to annoyance.

"*Xay!*" she screeched his nickname, the *Z* sound more pronounced in her exasperation.

Laughing harder, he backed away from the desk before she could take a swing at him.

"Sorry," he choked out, plopping down on the sofa affectionately known around the center as Yolanda's shrink's couch. "You know I couldn't resist."

"Obviously," she grumbled, shooting him an aggrieved look.

He grinned unrepentantly. "Now you know how Warrick,

Zeke and I felt when you used to barge into our room at the crack of dawn blasting 'Supersonic' on your radio. We *hated* that damn song."

Yolanda laughed. "Hey, don't blame me! Ma always sent me to wake y'all up for school. You guys were heavy sleepers, so I had to be creative." She sighed contentedly. "Good times."

"Yeah, whatever."

She grinned. "Don't you know it's unhealthy to hold grudges?"

"Says who? The author of that snoozer that put you to sleep?" Xavier teased, hitching his chin toward the thick psychology textbook lying open on her desk. Yolanda, who'd never had any serious aspirations to attend college, had not only earned a bachelor's degree while incarcerated, but was now working toward obtaining a master's in counseling psychology. With the fall semester underway, she had to divide her time between work, attending classes and completing her course assignments.

"I can't believe I dozed off." Yolanda arched her back, stretching her muscles as she yawned. "What time is it?"

Xavier flicked his wrist, consulting the gold watch that peeked from beneath the cuff of his white dress shirt. "It's after eleven."

Yolanda groaned. "I've still got a few more hours before it'll be safe to go home."

"Let me guess," Xavier said wryly. "Ma's hosting another one of her dinner parties."

"Unfortunately." Yolanda made a face. "I knew I wouldn't get any studying done if I stuck around the house. You know how Ma likes to parade us out to meet her friends. And even though she always hires an army of caterers and waitstaff, somehow Yasmin and I always get recruited into serving drinks and hors d'oeuvres."

Xavier chuckled, shaking his head at her. "So you

abandoned poor Yasmin. Just left her there to fend for herself. *Tsk-tsk.*"

Yolanda grinned. "She's the oldest," she said, referring to their sister who'd moved in with their mother after undergoing a nasty divorce. "She can take care of herself."

"By standing up to Ma?"

The two siblings looked at each other, then started chuckling at the thought of their mild-mannered sister taking on the indomitable force of nature that was Birdie Mayne.

"Anyway," Yolanda continued, "you're looking very *GQ* tonight. You must be on your way to the club to hang out with Zeke."

Sobering at once, Xavier murmured, "Not quite."

"Really? He called here about an hour ago looking for you. He was annoyed because he kept getting your voice mail." Yolanda rolled her eyes. "Of course he wanted you to know how many *fiiine* honeys you were missing out on meeting."

"Of course." Mouth twitching with wry humor, Xavier shook his head at his younger brother's womanizing reputation, which was legendary around town.

Yolanda was eyeing him curiously. "So if you're not meeting Zeke at the club, why are you all gussied up? Got a hot date?"

Xavier laughed shortly. "Not exactly."

"Then where did you go tonight?" Yolanda pressed. "Why didn't you answer any of Zeke's calls?" When Xavier didn't immediately respond, she leaned forward, her eyes filled with mounting curiosity. "Come on, Xay. The suspense is killing me."

Xavier hesitated another moment, then put his head back against the sofa and pushed out a deep breath. "I went to see Neveah."

He heard Yolanda gasp sharply. *"Neveah Symon?"*

A shadow of a smile touched Xavier's lips. "The one and only."

"Oh my God!" Yolanda exclaimed. "I thought she was living somewhere in Africa!"

"She was," Xavier confirmed, lifting his head to meet his sister's shocked stare. "But now she's back."

"When did she get back? And how did you find out? Did you run into her or something?"

Xavier chuckled, faintly amused by the rapid-fire questions. "She came home last week. And how I found out is still a mystery."

Yolanda frowned in confusion. "What do you mean?"

"Last week when I checked my mailbox, I found a postcard announcing an upcoming exhibit at Neveah's art gallery. There was a message written on the back of the card."

Yolanda was riveted. "What did it say?"

"It said, 'Neveah's coming home. If you want to see her, be there.' That's it. No name, no return address. Just the personalized message." He paused, remembering the range of emotions he'd experienced upon receiving the postcard. Shock. Elation. Anxiety. And, most of all, gratitude. Gratitude for the second chance he'd unexpectedly been given.

The rest of that day had been a blur. He'd tossed and turned all night, constantly waking up to switch on the nightstand lamp and reread the message on the postcard, although he'd already committed every word to memory. Until he arrived at the gallery this evening and saw Neveah with his own two eyes, he'd feared that someone was playing a cruel prank on him.

"Oh my God," Yolanda breathed, staring at him. "Did you recognize the handwriting?"

"No." He'd considered the possibility that Jordan was the anonymous sender. As co-owner of the art gallery, she was one of the few people who would have had access to the promotional postcards. But given their rancorous history, Xavier couldn't imagine Jordan going out of her way to notify him of Neveah's homecoming. When Neveah fled the country thirteen years ago, Jordan had adamantly refused to tell him where her best friend had gone, no matter how much he'd begged, cajoled and tried to reason with her. She'd stubbornly held her ground, telling him that he didn't deserve Neveah, that she was better off without him. And when he saw Jordan tonight at the gallery, she'd made it perfectly clear that her views hadn't changed. So he could safely assume that *she* wasn't the one who'd thrown him a lifeline by sending the postcard.

But if Jordan wasn't responsible, who was?

"So," Yolanda ventured, breaking into his thoughts, "how'd the reunion go?"

Xavier grimaced. "Not very well."

Yolanda's expression softened with sympathy. "So she wasn't happy to see you."

"*That's* an understatement. If she could have tossed me out on my ass without causing a scene, she probably would have."

"Damn." With a heavy sigh, Yolanda leaned back in her chair and shook her head at him. "You know, every time you came to visit me in prison, I kept expecting you to tell me that Neveah had returned home, and the two of you had worked things out and gotten back together. I mean, I was only fourteen when you guys started dating, but even *I* could see how crazy you were about each other. Ma used to worry that you and Neveah would run off and elope someday."

Xavier chuckled grimly. "Shows what Ma knows."

Yolanda searched his face. "So what was it like, seeing her again after all these years? How did she look?"

"Beautiful," Xavier murmured, reliving the moment he'd laid eyes on Neveah for the first time earlier that evening.

He'd been hovering near the entrance, pulse thudding as he scanned the crowd. And then he saw her. Standing alone in a corner and wearing a big, floppy hat that partially obscured her features as she studied a painting on the wall. But he hadn't needed to see her entire face to recognize her. Just the sight of her had tilted the ground beneath his feet, plunging him backward to a past he'd hoped to escape, yet needed desperately to recapture.

Heart pounding faster than a racehorse's, he'd made his way across the room toward her, wondering if she would disappear like a mirage once he reached her. But she hadn't. When he spoke her name, she'd turned around and lifted her head. The impact of those hauntingly familiar eyes locking onto his had nearly knocked him off his feet. He didn't know how long he'd stood there staring at her, hungrily devouring her smooth mocha skin and the gorgeous, heart-shaped face that featured finely sculpted cheekbones, an upturned nose, plush lips and a dimpled chin. He'd been struck by an overwhelming urge to drag her into his arms and kiss her so deeply and fiercely she wouldn't remember her own name, let alone their tumultuous past.

"Damn, Xay."

Yolanda's voice pulled him back to the present. Raising his eyes from the carpeted floor, he met her gentle, intuitive gaze.

"Still got it bad, don't you?" she murmured.

He swallowed tightly, then nodded. There was no use denying the truth.

Yolanda sighed. "So…what are you gonna do about it?"

"Whatever it takes," Xavier responded with quiet, steely determination.

And he meant every damn word.

Chapter 4

"Good morning."

Delores MacKay glanced up from the cup of herbal tea she'd been sipping to watch as Neveah padded into the large, sunny kitchen. She smiled warmly at her. "Good morning to you, too. I made you some coffee and an omelet."

"Great. Thanks, Mama." Neveah bent to kiss her mother's upturned cheek before crossing the room to retrieve a mug from the cabinet. After pouring herself some coffee, she added sugar and took a grateful sip.

"I hope the TV didn't wake you," her mother said, nodding toward the plasma television mounted on the wall, which was tuned to the gospel network she always watched whenever she missed Sunday service.

"Nope, didn't wake me at all. I was already up." Neveah refrained from adding that she'd hardly slept a wink last night, tortured by instant replays of her encounter with Xavier.

Xavier.

Dear God, had she really seen him last night? It seemed

utterly inconceivable. And yet, she knew it had been all too real.

"You're up earlier than I expected," Delores commented. "I thought you'd sleep in since you were out late last night. I tried to wait up for you, but I just couldn't keep my eyes open past ten."

Neveah grinned. "That's because you're getting old, Mama," she teased, although at sixty-one, Delores MacKay was *far* from elderly. With her glowing mahogany skin, keen dark eyes, full lips, long neck and graceful physique, she could have been a queen reincarnated from the soils of Africa. She wore her black hair in a short natural that sloped above her round forehead and accentuated the ethnic beauty of her features—a style that had inspired Neveah's own longer, fuller Afro.

But her mother's hair trends weren't *all* that had inspired Neveah over the years. As far as she was concerned, Delores MacKay was the smartest, strongest and most remarkable woman that had ever strutted across the face of the earth. Born and raised in the segregated South, Delores had felt the sting of social inequality from an early age, which drew her to participate in marches and boycotts as a young teenager. Fueled by the spirit of activism she'd harnessed during the sixties, she went on to become an outspoken civil rights attorney and activist. As a child, Neveah had been awed by her mother's ability to balance the demands of her career and motherhood. She'd successfully litigated cases in court, attended parent-teacher conferences, baked cakes for school fundraisers, served on community revitalization committees and organized protest rallies. But while Neveah may have been impressed with her mother's multitasking prowess, her father wasn't. Feeling neglected by his crusading wife, he'd started having affairs, brazenly flaunting his mistresses until Delores had had enough.

After enduring a bitter divorce and custody battle, and

devoting her entire career to championing the rights of others, Delores was now facing the biggest fight of her life. Three weeks ago, Neveah had been stunned when her mother called to share the devastating news that she'd been diagnosed with uterine cancer. Hearing the stark terror in her daughter's voice, Delores had hastened to explain that her doctors were extremely optimistic about her prognosis because the tumor had been detected early. Only slightly reassured, Neveah had waited until she'd hung up the phone before she broke down and bawled like a frightened baby. And then she'd packed up her small cottage, bid farewell to her friends and returned home immediately. As an only child, she would *never* forgive herself if something happened to her mother while she was living overseas.

"You're doing it again."

Neveah snapped back to the present. "Doing what?"

Delores sighed. "Ever since you arrived home a week ago, you've been hovering around me, staring at me as if you're afraid I'm going to keel over any minute."

Guilt assailed Neveah. "No, I haven't."

"Yes, you have. Why do you think I encouraged you to attend the reception last night? Since you've been back, you've hardly let me out of your sight. You've been following me around like a shadow, spending every waking minute you can with me. I've even woken up in the middle of the night to find that you've crawled into bed with me." She chuckled softly. "Don't get me wrong, sweetheart. I've always enjoyed your company and I'm grateful to have you back home. But I don't want you to stop living just because you think I'm dying. You need to get out more, visit some of your old friends. I don't want you hanging around, holding vigil at my bedside like a damn priest preparing to read my last rites."

Neveah swallowed a hard lump that had wedged in her

throat. "Fair enough," she grudgingly conceded. "But I *haven't* been staring at you like, like...what you said."

Delores gave her a look that told her this, too, was a lie.

Neveah said nothing more, ducking her head to sip her hot coffee. She knew her mother was right—she *had* been smothering her ever since she'd returned home. But she couldn't help it. Every time she thought about losing her mother, she was gripped by an overwhelming sense of despair. She couldn't imagine not having Delores MacKay in her life. Even though they'd lived on separate continents for the past thirteen years, the bond they shared had remained as strong as ever, nurtured by daily phone calls and Delores's twice-yearly visits to Senegal. Knowing that her proud, fiercely independent mother would resent being pitied or coddled, Neveah had endeavored to pretend that everything was normal. But, apparently, she was better at painting than acting.

"Your hair's getting long," Delores observed, changing the subject.

Absently Neveah reached up to touch the soft, springy hair that brushed her shoulders. For the past several years, she'd alternated between sporting an Afro and having her hair braided by a talented Senegalese woman. She'd taught Neveah how to moisturize and twist her hair into small sections, then comb out the locs to achieve the curly look she now wore.

Her mother gave her a teasingly affectionate smile. "You look a little like Erykah Badu with all that hair." Raising her mug to her lips, she surveyed Neveah's tie-dyed T-shirt, frayed denim cutoffs and brown suede moccasins. "My bohemian baby. Where are you off to this morning?"

Neveah sighed dramatically. "Well, since you're so eager to be rid of me—"

Delores rolled her eyes heavenward.

"—I'm heading back to the gallery," Neveah finished, crossing to the center island and sliding onto the stool beside her mother's. "There's a large storage room that I want to clear out and use as my studio. I figured now's the perfect time to tackle the job since the gallery is closed for Labor Day weekend."

Delores nodded. "Is Jordan going to help you?"

"Nope. She's on her way to South Padre Island to enjoy a few days of fun and sun on the beach." Neveah grinned wryly. "She said she'll send me a postcard."

"I bet she will," Delores murmured, sipping her tea.

Neveah pretended not to hear the trace of mockery in her mother's voice. Although Neveah and Jordan had been best friends since college, Delores MacKay had never completely warmed to Jordan, treating her with a polite reserve that had baffled and frustrated Neveah. Once, when she'd asked her mother outright why she seemed to dislike Jordan so much, Delores had cradled her face between her hands, peered somberly into her eyes and whispered a proverb in Wolof, the most common regional language spoken in Senegal.

When Neveah asked for a translation, Delores had smiled enigmatically. "One day, when you travel to Senegal to continue the work of tracing our family's roots, you can ask someone to tell you the meaning of my words."

Unnerved and confused by her mother's cryptic response, Neveah had never broached the subject again.

"So," Delores began conversationally, "how did the reception go last night?"

"It went really well. Great turnout." Neveah drank her coffee, deliberately avoiding her mother's inquisitive gaze. She'd already decided not to tell her about Xavier's unexpected appearance at the gallery last night. Next to Jordan, no one knew better than Delores how Xavier's betrayal had nearly destroyed Neveah. Delores had been so worried about her daughter's emotional state that she'd taken an extended leave of absence from her law firm and traveled to Senegal to look after Neveah for four months. Now, with her own health in the balance, the *last* thing she needed to be worrying about was Neveah's troubled love life.

"Did anyone recognize you?" Delores prodded.

"Not at all," Neveah lied with a straight face. "Jordan's hat disguise really worked."

"I see," Delores murmured into her cup. "Well, I guess if anyone knows a thing or two about wearing disguises, Jordan would."

Neveah heaved an exasperated breath. "Ma—"

"While you're eating your breakfast," Delores interrupted, "I'll take a shower and get dressed so I can accompany you to the gallery. I want to help you clear out that storage room and get your studio ready so you'll have somewhere to paint."

Before she'd even finished speaking, Neveah was shaking her head. "You'll do no such thing."

"And why not?" Delores demanded, setting down her mug. "I'm fully capable of—"

"Mama, you're having major surgery in a month. You're supposed to be resting your body, not taking on strenuous manual labor."

"Nonsense. If I'm dying, lifting and carrying some boxes isn't going to hasten my demise."

"Mama!" Neveah cried, aghast. "That's not funny!"

"Oh, hush. You know what I meant. And I've already told you I'm not dying. My doctor has all but staked his medical license on my survival. So I'm not going anywhere."

"Exactly. And you're not coming to the gallery with me, either," Neveah stated firmly.

Delores scowled. "But you need help, and I—"

"—can stay here and wait until I return." Neveah cut her mother a warning look. "Don't forget that I can be *just* as stubborn as you are."

"As if I could ever forget," Delores grumbled.

After several tense moments, Neveah leaned over and rested her head on her mother's shoulder. "I won't be gone all day. When I come back from the gallery, we can go to your favorite Caribbean restaurant and stuff our faces. How does that sound?"

"Sounds just fine." Delores calmly picked up her mug of tea. "Which is why I already called and made reservations."

Neveah gaped at her mother for a moment, then burst out laughing.

An hour later, she was pulling into the art gallery's empty parking lot when her cell rang. She grabbed the phone from the console, glanced at the caller ID and grinned when she saw Jordan's number. Pressing the talk button, she said wryly, "Don't tell me you're already calling to rub it in."

"Rub what in?"

"The fact that you're on your way to the beach while *I'm* stuck clearing out the storage room."

"Oh. That." Jordan laughed. "Now why would I brag about spending a few days on the beach when you actually *lived* on a beach for several years?"

Neveah chuckled. "Good point. So what's up?"

"Are you at the gallery yet?"

"Just got here. Why?"

Jordan hesitated. "I need a huge favor. I was just checking our voice mail—"

Neveah tsk-tsked. "Such a workaholic."

"I know, I know. But I'm glad I checked the voice mail, because there was an urgent message from one of our buyers who attended the showing last night. She purchased your *Golden Ecstasy* painting, which, you may recall, was the most expensive piece on display last night."

"Mmm-hmm. So what did her message say? Does she want her money back?"

Jordan laughed. "Of course not! Actually, she wants the painting delivered to her sooner than we'd anticipated."

"Oh? How soon?"

"Uhhh," Jordan hedged. "Today?"

Neveah frowned, pausing with her hand on the car door handle. "But today's Sunday. Unless I'm mistaken, we don't do deliveries on Sundays."

"You're right. We don't. But considering how much this woman just spent on your painting, I figured I'd make an exception this time. But here's the thing. I haven't been able to reach our driver, so I've been calling every delivery service in town. But since it's Labor Day weekend, no one's available until Tuesday."

"Can't the buyer wait until then?"

"Apparently not. Her husband's coming home early from a business trip, and she wants to surprise him by having the painting already hung up in their bedroom." Jordan snickered. "You *did* say you were inspired by lust when you created it."

Neveah grinned wryly. "The buyer wouldn't happen to be Margot Rosenblum, would it?"

"No," Jordan said laughingly. "And thanks for the mental picture. Anyway, what I've been trying to get at—"

"—is that you want *me* to deliver the painting," Neveah concluded.

"Would you?" Jordan asked, as if the idea had only just occurred to her. "That would be *wonderful,* Neveah. And just imagine how excited the buyer's going to be when *you* show up on her doorstep! How many art collectors can say they've had paintings personally delivered to them by the artist? I bet Seth could find a way to spin this into a fabulous public-relations piece."

"Considering that I'm not supposed to show my face in

public for another two weeks," Neveah drolly reminded Jordan, "we might want to keep this to ourselves."

"Good point. So you'll do it? You'll deliver the painting?"

Neveah hesitated. She couldn't deny a sudden curiosity to meet the buyer who'd purchased her latest portrait. As an artist, Neveah poured her heart and soul into every work of art she produced, spending many sleepless nights to bring her creative vision to life on canvas. After applying the final brushstroke, she always felt a certain sentimentality about parting with the completed piece. She'd often likened the sale of her paintings to giving up a child for adoption.

"Neveah?" Jordan prompted.

She wavered, gazing longingly at the entrance to the gallery. "I don't know. I really wanted to get started on that storage room."

"I'll help you when I get back," Jordan promised. "And so will Chelsea. You shouldn't have to tackle that project by yourself anyway."

Neveah hesitated another moment, then relented with a deep sigh. "All right. I'll do it."

"Oh, thank God! Thank you *so* much, Neveah."

"Yeah, yeah, yeah. I guess this is what you meant about putting me right to work, huh? At this rate," she joked, "we might not even be on speaking terms by the end of the week."

After a prolonged silence, Jordan murmured, "You have no idea."

Chapter 5

Seated behind the wheel of a white delivery van emblazoned with the art gallery's logo, Neveah gazed out the window at ripened green pastures dotted with grazing cattle and horses. According to Jordan's directions, the buyer lived fifty miles outside of Houston in a rural area named Cat Spring. As Neveah traveled down the two-lane highway, she couldn't help admiring the passing scenery. As much as she'd enjoyed Senegal's tropical climate and stunningly beautiful beaches, she'd missed the vivid blue skies and wide-open spaces of her native Texas. She'd stayed away for thirteen years, drawing strength and healing from the land of her African ancestors. But on some spiritual level, she'd always known she could never escape the call of home. Home was where the heart was.

So her home would always be Texas.

Minutes after turning down a narrow country road, Neveah drove through an open gated entrance and followed the curve of the paved driveway until she reached her destination—a large single-story stone ranch house that overlooked a lake and rested on at least one hundred acres of lush, rolling terrain.

Whistling softly under her breath, Neveah passed two smaller outbuildings and a detached carport before pulling up to the main house. She climbed out of the van slowly, utterly enchanted by the natural beauty of her surroundings. The buyer not only had excellent taste in art, she mused, but in homes, as well.

Smiling to herself, she headed to the back of the van to open the rear double doors. Since the painting had already been wrapped, all she'd had to do was load it into the delivery van. Framed in gold leaf, the piece was heavy, but Jordan had assured her that one of the buyer's household servants would be on hand to carry the painting to the master bedroom.

When Neveah heard the front door opening and closing, she stepped around the side of the van.

And froze.

Sauntering toward her, looking outrageously sexy in a plain white T-shirt, low-slung blue jeans and dusty leather boots, was none other than Xavier Mayne.

Stunned into speechlessness, Neveah could only gape at him as he approached, munching on what appeared to be a peach. His dark eyes swept over her, taking in her curly Afro and the deep V of her T-shirt before sliding down to her bare thighs. His gaze lingered long enough to set her skin ablaze before his eyes returned to her flushed face. He gave her a slow, crooked smile, and *damn* if her heart rate didn't quadruple.

"Hey, beautiful," he murmured.

Neveah glared up at him, hands thrust onto her hips. "Don't 'Hey, beautiful' me. What the hell's going on here? Jordan didn't tell me *you* were the buyer!"

His lips quirked. "That was the general idea." He took

another bite of the peach, then handed it to her. "Hold this for me."

She sputtered with indignation as he closed her fingers around the plump, dewy peach. "Don't drop it," he warned, turning toward the van, "or I'll make you walk to the farmer's market up the road to get me some more."

Neveah eyed him incredulously. "Are you out of your damn mind? You can't *make* me do anything! And I really don't appreciate being tricked into—" She broke off midrant as he reached inside the van and lifted out the painting. His thick, muscular biceps flexed with the motion, and his jeans hugged his firm, round butt.

Her mouth ran dry.

She watched as he closed the van's doors and started toward the house, carrying the heavy painting as though it weighed no more than an Etch A Sketch.

When Neveah didn't follow him, he glanced over his shoulder at her. "Coming?"

"I don't think so," she said tartly. "I did my part by delivering the painting. You're on your own."

He gave her a long, measuring look.

She glared back defiantly.

An amused gleam lit his eyes. "Could you at least bring my peach?"

Neveah glanced down at the piece of fruit in her hand as if she'd forgotten how it got there.

"Please?" Xavier prompted softly.

Neveah held his gaze for another moment, then huffed out an exasperated breath and stalked after him, sorely tempted to hurl the peach at the back of his head like a baseball. God knows he deserved a good thunking. Where in the world did he get off pulling an outrageous stunt like this? And how on earth had he convinced Jordan to go along with it?

Temper simmering, Neveah followed him up the driveway

toward the house, which was shaded by tall, leafy oaks and boasted a wraparound porch that was perfect for gathering to enjoy quiet conversations after dinner. Without warning, her mind conjured an image of her and Xavier rocking gently on the porch swing and holding hands as they watched the sun set over the lake.

Shaken by the thought, and dismayed by the sharp pang of longing that accompanied it, Neveah frowned, absently biting into the peach. As the sweet, succulent juices bathed her taste buds, she made an appreciative sound that drew Xavier's amused gaze.

"Good, isn't it?"

"Mmmm." She couldn't resist taking another bite, so distracted by her enjoyment of the luscious peach that she didn't realize she'd followed Xavier into the house until he closed the door behind her. And then she was too busy admiring the gorgeous interior to remember that she'd never actually intended to cross the threshold.

Her stunned gaze swept from the dramatically high ceilings to the ceramic tile floors that flowed into an enormous living room, which featured crown molding, a soaring limestone fireplace and solid, rustic furnishings done in rich earth tones. Everywhere she looked, there seemed to be walls of windows that offered sweeping views of the surrounding terrain. She couldn't see another house for miles.

"Wow," she whispered. "This is quite a place."

"Thanks," Xavier responded with a lazy smile. "I'm glad you like it. Be right back."

She watched as he disappeared down the hallway, carrying the painting to wherever he'd decided to hang it. Idly munching on the peach, she advanced into the living room, lured by the broad expanse of windows. As she gazed across the green valley, she could visualize the fields blanketed with a vibrant palette of Texas wildflowers during the springtime. In her mind's eye, she painted a lush meadow of bluebonnets, bright Indian paintbrushes, deep pink winecups and crimson wild poppies.

"I've missed that look."

Startled, Neveah turned from the window to find Xavier standing across the room, watching her with an expression of tender yearning.

Her heart thudded. "W-what look?"

"The look you have when something has inspired you. When you're creating one of your masterpieces. It's a look of pure rapture." He smiled quietly. "I've missed it."

Blushing, Neveah gestured outside. "I was just admiring the beautiful view."

"It's even more beautiful in the spring, when the wildflowers are in bloom." He paused. "You'll have to come back and paint it."

She wanted to. *Oh,* how she wanted to. And she shouldn't have.

"How long have you lived here?" she asked abruptly.

"Five years," he answered. "I bought the ranch as an investment property, then decided to make it my home instead."

"I can definitely see why. It's prime real estate. But it's a bit out of the way for you, isn't it? Your commute into the city must be an hour, at least."

He shrugged one broad shoulder. "It's worth the sacrifice."

"Really?" Her tone was mockingly skeptical. "What about your friends? How do *they* feel about having to drive all the way out here for your fabulous parties?"

"Makes no difference to me." His gaze shifted to the window, his expression clouding for a moment. "I needed a change of scenery."

Neveah sobered, sensing pain beneath the surface of his

veiled response. She thought of his embattled childhood, remembering how the specter of his father's desertion had haunted him throughout their relationship. She found herself wondering whether things could have worked out differently between them, if only—

She frowned, giving herself a hard mental shake. *No.* She would not go down that road again. She knew all too well what awaited her at the end.

And on that note…

"I should get going," she announced.

"Not yet," Xavier said. "I was hoping you could help me out with something."

"What?"

He started toward her, moving with that lazy, rolling swagger she'd never forgotten, no matter how hard she'd tried. His dark gaze pinned her to the floor where she stood, completely immobile, heart slamming against her rib cage.

When he reached her, her eyes lowered to trace the wide breadth of his shoulders, and up again to the strong column of his throat, the rugged curve of his jaw, the lush fullness of his mouth. She lingered there, reliving the memory of those soft lips moving against hers, remembering the way he could always command her surrender with just one searing kiss.

As a familiar ache of longing curled through her, she raised her eyes to his face, meeting his gaze. A current of pure sexual awareness passed between them.

He shifted closer. "What're you thinking about?"

Her stomach quivered at the deep, husky timbre of his voice. "I was thinking about you—" she saw his pupils darken before she added "—and how different you look."

"I *am* different," he said quietly.

"So I've noticed. You've exchanged your downtown bachelor pad for a remote country ranch. You shop at farmers' markets instead of corner drugstores. You're not wearing so much as a stitch of jewelry." She smiled wryly. "I'd say you've *definitely* changed."

"I've changed in other ways, too." His voice deepened meaningfully. "Ways that truly matter."

She stared into his dark eyes, afraid to believe what he was telling her. Afraid to hope.

"I've also gotten better at sharing." Lips twitching with humor, he glanced pointedly at the remnants of the peach she held.

Following the direction of his gaze, Neveah grinned sheepishly. "Sorry. I couldn't help myself. It was absolutely delicious."

He smiled. "I know."

"Here." She held out the peach. "I left you a few good bites."

He didn't reach for the proffered fruit. Instead, holding her gaze, he lowered his head to her hand. She watched, mesmerized, as his straight white teeth sank into the plump, moist flesh of the peach.

"Mmm," he rumbled, chewing slowly. "Tastes even better than I remembered."

She shivered, need gathering low in her belly. She stared at his full, glistening lips as he bent and took another bite, his eyes slanting closed in an expression of ecstasy.

Neveah smothered a groan.

When juice oozed from the peach and trickled down the inside of her wrist, he murmured, "I'll get that."

Her breath escaped on a soft gasp as he ran his tongue down her arm, chasing the rivulet of juice. Her nipples hardened and her clitoris swelled with arousal. Her fingers reflexively tightened around the peach as he slowly licked his way down to her elbow. The sensual stroke of his tongue made wetness leak from her sex faster than the juices dripping from the fruit.

When he began sucking gently at a pulsing nerve, the peach fell limply from her hand, landing on the floor with a dull thud. The sound echoed loudly around the room, snapping her back to sanity.

With a strangled gasp, she snatched her tingling arm away and took a hasty step backward.

Xavier gazed at her from beneath his thick, dark lashes. "Neveah—"

"I—I have to go." Heart hammering, she sidestepped him and hurried from the room.

"Neveah, wait." He started after her. "We need to talk—"

"No, we don't!"

"Yes, we do, damn it."

She flung open the front door and charged onto the porch just as he reached her, grabbing her upper arm to forestall her escape. "You can't keep running—"

That did it.

Wrenching her arm out of his grasp, Neveah rounded furiously on him and exploded, "Damn you! Who do you think you are? As if it weren't bad enough that you showed up at my art gallery last night, expecting me to welcome you with open arms—"

He frowned. "I didn't expect—"

"—but then you had the *audacity* to trick me into delivering a painting to you! Did you think I would forget all about the past just because you spent a small fortune on my artwork? Is that it? Or did you think I would want you back simply because you've spent a few years altering your lifestyle? Which is it, Xavier?"

"Neither."

"Then what is it?" she demanded, choking with outrage. "What makes you think, even for a second, that I want you back in my life? You *hurt* me, Xavier. Not once, not twice— *repeatedly!* Every time I needed you, you went missing in

action! Between your immature buddies and the constant procession of women who were supposedly 'just friends,' I never knew where I ranked on your list of priorities. I supported you in everything—*everything!*—but I can count on one hand the number of my art exhibits you even bothered to attend while I was in college. Am I supposed to be *grateful* that you showed up last night and bought one of my paintings? Give me a damn break!"

He stared at her, his dark eyes glittering with raw emotion. "I'm not disputing anything you've said—"

"Because you can't!"

He snapped his mouth shut and hung his head, a muscle throbbing in his clenched jaw.

Neveah glared at him, chest heaving with fury. She hated him for doing this to her, for barging back into her life and pouring acid into the raw, festering wound over her heart that stubbornly refused to heal. Why couldn't he have stayed away from her? *Why, God?*

"I know how much I hurt you, Neveah," he began in a low, humble voice. "I know I wasn't half the man you needed or deserved. I took you for granted because I was too selfish and immature to appreciate what I had. But believe me when I tell you that I've *always* loved you. I loved you back then," he said, his eyes boring deep into hers, "and I'll love you till the day I die. Believe that."

Neveah's throat seized as though she'd suffered a blow to her solar plexus. She averted her gaze, blinking back tears of pain, anger and sorrow.

He edged closer. "Whether you like it or not, Neveah, we have unfinished business. Now that you're back home, I'm going to do everything in my power to prove to you that we belong together. And make no mistake about it, sweetheart. We *do* belong together."

Neveah's incredulous gaze swung back to him. "Let me

explain something to you, since I obviously didn't make myself clear last night *or* just now. I don't want anything to do with you. You represent an excruciatingly painful chapter of my life that I'd rather not revisit. So I'm telling you for the last time. *Leave. Me. Alone.*"

Xavier shook his head, holding her gaze unflinchingly. "I'm not going away."

"No?" she jeered. "Well, *I* am."

With that, she spun on her heel and stalked off toward the delivery van.

This time, he made no move to follow her.

Chapter 6

As Neveah reached the van, she dug inside her pocket for the keys. When she came up empty-handed, she patted down her back pockets. Nothing.

Frowning, she looked inside the van to see whether she'd left the keys in the ignition. But, no, she couldn't have. She'd needed them to unlock the rear doors.

With a deepening frown, she headed to the back of the van and peered through the window. To her utter dismay, the keys were lying right there on the backseat.

She groaned loudly, slapping a hand to her forehead. She remembered setting them down when she'd opened the rear doors to retrieve the painting. Moments later, she'd been so flustered by Xavier's appearance that she'd forgotten to pick up the keys before he closed the van's doors.

"Damn him!" Neveah hissed.

She tried the door handle, but of course it was locked. Since the delivery van was used to transport valuable artwork, it was equipped with an antitheft alarm system, which meant even the back doors locked automatically. She'd have to call a tow truck.

But there was just one problem.

She'd locked her handbag—along with her cell phone— inside the van, as well.

"Shit, shit, shit," Neveah swore under her breath. She'd have to swallow her pride and ask Xavier if she could use his phone.

Absolutely dreading the task, she squared her shoulders, stalked around the van and headed toward the house. She grew even more incensed at the sight of Xavier reclining on the wooden porch swing, his arms draped over the back as he lazily rocked back and forth. There was no mistaking the wicked gleam in his eyes as he watched her approach.

"Something wrong?" he called out with exaggerated concern.

Neveah scowled at him. "Like *you* don't know."

He blinked innocently. "Beg your pardon?"

"My keys are locked in the van." Stopping at the bottom of the porch steps, she planted her hands on her hips and glared up at him. "Didn't you see them sitting there before you closed the doors?"

"Nope."

Her eyes narrowed suspiciously. "You sure about that?"

He gave her an affronted look. "Are you implying that I deliberately locked your keys in the van to keep you stranded here?"

"Did you?"

He laughed, a deep, rich, masculine rumble that made her belly clench. The infuriating man was too damn sexy for his own good.

"I didn't sabotage you, Neveah," he told her. "But I'd be lying if I said I'm not pleased that you're stuck here. We didn't finish our discussion."

"Yes, we did," she said tightly. "Anyway, I need to use your phone to call a tow truck."

"You don't need a tow truck," Xavier said lazily.

"No? You got a spare key to the van I don't know about?"

"Don't need one. I can get the door unlocked for you."

"Really?" Even as Neveah asked, she was transported back to the day they'd first met, when he'd hot-wired her mother's car for Neveah when she had lost the keys.

"I'd really appreciate it if you could get the door unlocked for me," she said now, though her pride balked at having to request *anything* of him.

The amused gleam in his eyes told her he knew it, too. "As you may recall, I can definitely help you out with that."

"Thanks, that'd be—"

"But then again," he amended, his eyes narrowing thoughtfully as he assessed the van in the driveway, "that's a newer model."

"So?"

"So," he explained, "most cars built after the eighties were designed to resist wire hangers and slim jims. You know, to protect owners from theft. Since your van is a newer model, I could actually damage the lock if I tried to jimmy it. And that'd be a real shame. So maybe you *do* need to call a tow truck or a locksmith. Of course, with this being Labor Day weekend—and given how remote my ranch is—it could be a while before someone shows up." He paused, his eyes glinting with satisfaction. "A *long* while."

As his meaning registered, Neveah glared venomously at him. "What do you want?" she asked through gritted teeth.

"You know what I want," he murmured.

"No."

"I want to finish our discussion."

"*No.*"

"Is that your final answer?"

"Yes."

He shrugged. "Suit yourself."

As she watched, he clasped his hands behind his head and crossed his big, booted feet at the ankles, posturing like he had all the time in the world. Her temper flared, even as she found herself reluctantly admiring the way the fabric of his T-shirt stretched across his wide, muscular chest and ridged abdomen.

Swallowing hard, she glowered at him. "This is ridiculous, Xavier. It's *your* fault that I'm stranded out here. Not only did you lure me out here under false pretenses, but then you locked my keys in the van. The least you could do is let me use your damn phone."

"I'd be more than happy to," he said mildly. "*After* we talk."

Neveah heaved an exasperated breath, all but stamping her foot like a child throwing a temper tantrum. "I already told you we have *nothing* to talk about!"

"Wrong answer." He continued swaying gently on the porch swing.

Neveah spat a curse in Wolof.

He grinned wickedly. "What was that you said? I don't speak that language."

"I *said*," she ground out, "I'm listening."

When he crooked his finger at her, she felt like Eve being beckoned into temptation by the devil himself. God knows Xavier Mayne had already caused her downfall once before.

"Come here," he murmured.

Her pulse drummed erratically. "I can hear you just fine from where I'm standing."

Shaking his head, he patted the spot next to him on the swing. "Come. Sit."

Knowing she had no other choice, Neveah sighed harshly and stomped up the porch steps. Deliberately ignoring the spot he'd indicated, she sat down at the opposite end of the swing and angrily folded her arms across her chest.

Xavier chuckled softly, amused by her show of defiance. His dark eyes wandered over her bare legs, following the shapely curve of her thighs down to her toned calves. The heat of his gaze scorched her nerve endings and caused a heavy, throbbing warmth to settle in her loins. She resisted the urge to squirm or tug at her shorts, refusing to let him see just how much he affected her.

"I'm here," she snapped. "So talk."

Those sensual lips twitched. "What's the rush?"

"For your information," she said curtly, "I have things to do."

"Like what?"

She bristled. "Excuse me?"

"You said you have things to do. What kind of things?" When she scowled, he added quietly, "I'm not questioning whether you're telling the truth. I'm asking because I'm curious about you. Curious about your life."

She faltered for a moment, disarmed by the gentle sincerity in his voice and the vulnerability she'd glimpsed in his eyes. Despite the fact that she'd earned the right to behave like a bitch toward him, to rant and rave and scream profanities at him, she felt an unwelcome twinge of guilt that made her respond in a less combative tone, "I was planning to clear out some storage space at the gallery."

Xavier nodded. "You need somewhere to paint."

"Yes." She was surprised—and reluctantly pleased—that he'd made the correct assumption.

"Will that be private enough for you? Being at the gallery?"

She'd actually wondered the same thing. "I hope so. I could

look for studio space to rent, but I really don't have time to go driving around town to check out different places. Anyway, I should be fine at the gallery. My studio will be tucked all the way in the back, and Jordan will make sure no one disturbs me while I'm working."

As she spoke, Xavier's eyes roamed across her face in a slow, lazy perusal. "Have I already told you," he said huskily, "how absolutely beautiful you look?"

Caught off guard by the compliment, Neveah blushed from head to toe. "Xavier—"

"It's true. I can't take my eyes off you, Neveah. And I really like your hair this way. It suits you perfectly."

"Thanks," she murmured, her insides tingling with pleasure. "I haven't straightened my hair in years. It's been incredibly liberating."

"That's good." He kept staring at her, his eyes devouring her with a hunger that made her pulse go haywire.

Forcing herself to glance away, she drew a shaky breath and discreetly wiped her damp palms on her shorts. "How's your family?" she asked, deliberately changing the subject.

"Everyone's doing well," Xavier said warmly. "Warrick and Raina just had a baby boy. Well, not *just*. Little War's six months old now."

"Really? That's wonder—" Neveah broke off abruptly, eyes narrowing. "Wait a minute. Raina who?"

Xavier grinned. "Raina St. James."

Neveah's jaw went slack. "You mean Yolanda's quiet little friend? *That* Raina?"

"Yep." His grin widened. "Shocked the hell out of the rest of us, too. Turns out she'd had a secret crush on War for years."

Neveah chuckled, thinking of Xavier's darkly handsome older brother. "That's not surprising. Everyone had the hots for Warrick."

Xavier frowned, lifting a brow at her. "Present company excluded, right?"

"Well…" At his thunderous scowl, she laughed. "Relax. I'm just teasing you."

"Yeah, okay," he grumbled, and for one crazy moment, she wished she could lean over and kiss his soft, sensual lips to show him just why she'd only had eyes for him.

Which was why it was time for her to go.

Clearing her throat, she glanced pointedly at her wristwatch. "You said you wanted to talk…" she prompted.

"We are." He smiled indolently, setting the swing in motion again. "How's your mama doing?"

Neveah stiffened, then answered neutrally, "She's doing fine."

She didn't tell him about her mother's condition. She didn't want his pity or concern, and confiding such a deeply personal matter would only open the door to more sharing and intimacy between them—which was the *last* thing she needed.

"Is she still practicing law?" Xavier asked.

Neveah nodded. Her mother hadn't missed a day of work since being diagnosed with cancer. Interacting with her colleagues and clients kept her busy and helped take her mind off her health crisis.

"And what about your father? When was the last time you saw him?"

Neveah smiled faintly. "Last Christmas. He and my stepmother visited me in Senegal." Although her parents' marriage had ended acrimoniously, Neveah had long since forgiven her father for cheating on her mother and destroying their family. He'd made a terrible mistake, but even Delores would be the first to admit that she was as much to blame for the divorce as he was. And no one could dispute that Langley Symon had always been a good father to Neveah. Even after losing custody of her and moving to California, he'd remained part of her life, never missing birthdays or holidays, and sending for her several times a year. But as much as Neveah loved her father, she couldn't bear the thought of him being her only surviving parent.

Shaking off the gloomy thought, she smiled wryly at Xavier. "Have we done enough 'talking' yet?"

He shook his head slowly. "Not by a long shot."

Her smile faded. "You *do* know you can't keep me here forever, don't you? I have dinner reservations with my mom. If I'm not back in time, she'll file a missing person's report with the police." Even as the words left her mouth, she remembered her mother admonishing her to get out more. She wondered what Delores would think if she knew where Neveah was, and whom she was with.

Xavier chuckled. "Relax, sweetheart. I'm not going to kidnap you." He paused. "Not that the thought hasn't crossed my mind."

Neveah shot him a dark glance, and he laughed.

Sobering after a few moments, he said, "What I wanted to talk to you about involves the community center."

"The one you founded with your brothers?"

"That's right." He sounded surprised that she knew about it.

She gave him a sardonic look. "Even before your little girlfriend mentioned it last night—"

He frowned. "She's not my girlfriend."

"—I'd already heard about it through an article I read. My mom sent me a link to the story when the community center first opened seven years ago. We were both very impressed with the center's mission to provide a safe haven for at-risk youth from the Third Ward." Neveah hesitated, then added with quiet sincerity, "I'm proud of you and your siblings for giving back to our old community and making such a huge difference in the lives of so many children."

Xavier shrugged, seemingly embarrassed by her praise. "We just wanted them to have something we didn't when we were growing up. Believe me," he added with a chuckle, "we get as much enjoyment out of the facilities as the kids do."

Neveah smiled softly, touched by his attempt to downplay the tremendous generosity of the gift he and his brothers had bestowed upon the community. Deciding to play along, she teased, "So I suppose *you* don't really do much as executive director. You're probably just a figurehead, huh?"

"Absolutely." His eyes glimmered with amusement. "A glorified paper pusher."

Neveah laughed. And then, because it felt perfectly natural, she nudged off her moccasins, drew her legs up to her chest and angled her body on the swing to face him. He rewarded her with a warm smile that melted her insides.

A mild summer breeze rustled the leaves of the surrounding canopy of trees that shaded the house. Neveah breathed deeply, inhaling the scents of earth and lush vegetation. Lulled by the gentle rocking motions of the swing, she felt a dreamy languor steal over her senses. Although she fought to resist the hypnotic spell of the place, she found herself reliving the vision she'd had of her and Xavier swaying together on the swing as they watched the sun set over the lake. Suddenly she wanted to crawl into his lap, find her favorite resting place on his shoulder, close her eyes and drift off to sleep.

"So here's the thing." Xavier's lazy drawl had the consistency of thick, melting molasses. "I want to commission an artist to paint a mural inside the community center. Something with an inspirational message. Something that serves as a daily reminder of the spirit of unity, hope and perseverance we're trying to foster among our youth."

Neveah nodded, blinking slowly. "I think I understand what you're looking for."

"Good." He looked into her eyes. "Because I think you're the perfect artist to bring my vision to life."

Dragged out of her somnolent trance, Neveah stared at him. "Are you saying you want *me* to paint the mural?"

"That's exactly what I'm saying."

She shook her head in swift refusal. "I'm flattered that you thought of me, Xavier, but I'm afraid I can't help you. But I know many talented artists who would jump at such an opportunity. I'd be more than happy to recommend—"

"There's no one I'd trust more than you to do justice to this mural." His gaze turned gently imploring. "Please reconsider, Neveah."

She hesitated, not entirely immune to the appeal of the project. She, too, had grown up in the Third Ward, and although her paintings had garnered her fame and fortune beyond her wildest dreams, she'd never forgotten where she came from. Through her gallery, she'd established a minority scholarship program that enabled low-income students to attend prestigious art schools around the country. She also belonged to several community organizations and had taught art to young children while living in Senegal. She'd always welcomed opportunities to give back to her community any way she could.

Until now.

"I'm sorry," she said with another shake of her head. "I can't."

"I know what you're worth," Xavier pressed. "You'd be more than well compensated for—"

She frowned. "It's not about the money, and you know it."

He grew silent for a minute, his dark eyes probing hers. "So it's about us, then. About the past."

Neveah gave him an incredulous look. "Do you even have to ask?"

"You wouldn't be doing this for me, Neveah. You'd be doing it for the community."

"Doesn't matter," she said, ignoring the sharp stab of guilt that pricked her conscience. "I can't work with you, Xavier."

"You wouldn't be working with me. You wouldn't even have to see me very often. I know we were joking a minute ago about me being a glorified paper pusher, but the truth is that my executive director duties keep me pretty damn busy. I serve on so many different boards and committees, I practically need two assistants just to keep my schedule straight. If I'm not attending one meeting or another, I'm sequestered in my office, buried to my ears in paperwork. So I'd definitely be out of your way. And the area where you'd be painting will be closed to the public until the unveiling. So you could work in peace any hour of the day or night."

"Sorry," Neveah said firmly. "I can't help you."

He leaned forward, his gaze intent upon her face. "Just give it some thought. Can you at least do that for me?"

A surge of resentment flashed through her. "You have no right to ask *anything* of me."

He sighed heavily. "I know—"

"Obviously you don't." Angrily she swung her legs down to the floor, shoved her feet into her moccasins and stood up.

Xavier frowned at her. "Where are you going?"

"Since you insist on holding me hostage," she snapped, "I'm going to walk down to one of your neighbor's houses and ask to use *their* damn phone."

"Good luck with that," Xavier drawled, mouth twitching as he leaned back against the swing. "The closest property isn't for another twenty miles."

Standing at the edge of the porch, Neveah surveyed the vast rolling terrain surrounding them and scowled. She knew he was right, and she didn't relish the idea of striking out on her own down some backwoods country road. God knows *where* she'd end up.

Whirling around, she jabbed a finger at her captor and raged, "Xavier Maximillian Mayne, if you don't march into that house *right* now and get me your damn phone, I swear to—"

"Okay, okay. Damn. No need to resort to calling out middle names—especially *that* one." With a mock shudder, Xavier rolled to his feet with a fluidity that defied his powerful build. "I'll be right back. Don't go anywhere."

She smirked. "As if."

He chuckled softly.

As he turned and opened the screen door, she heard a phone ringing somewhere inside the house. Moments later she heard the deep timbre of his voice, followed by his laughter. She frowned, concluding that the caller *had* to be a woman. Probably Alyson, calling to find out what time he was picking her up for their date—which they'd undoubtedly arranged seconds after Neveah left them alone last night.

Unnerved by the thought, she crept closer to the front door, torturing herself with mental images of Xavier sharing one of his luscious peaches with Alyson, slowly licking his way down *her* arm—

"All right, Alyson," she heard him say, confirming her suspicion about the identity of his caller. "See you then."

Neveah's stomach plunged. She moved away from the front door before he caught her eavesdropping on his conversation.

A minute later he emerged from the house. Instead of his cell phone, he held a long metal object that she recognized as a slim jim.

She frowned. "I thought you said you could damage my lock if you used one of those."

Striding past her, he muttered, "It's possible."

"Then why are you using it?" she demanded, following him off the porch and down the driveway.

"Do you want to leave or not?"

"Absolutely." She hesitated, then couldn't resist adding casually, "But I just find it rather interesting that after holding me captive all this time, you're suddenly in a hurry to get rid of me. Got a hot date or something?"

He chuckled. "I'm not in a hurry to get rid of you, Neveah. If I could keep you here forever, I would."

Any pleasure she may have derived from his response was neutralized by the fact that he hadn't denied having a date.

"Unless you'd rather wait hours for a tow truck to show up—" he held up the metal tool in his hand "—this is the quickest way to get you back on the road. That *is* what you want, isn't it?"

"Of course." But her voice suddenly lacked conviction.

As they reached the driver's side of the van, Xavier suddenly paused and looked down at her. "What're you doing tomorrow for Labor Day?"

She hesitated. "Nothing. Why?"

"We're having our annual Labor Day picnic at the community center. It's open to the public, and it's always a pretty popular event. Live bands, carnival rides, fireworks and all the barbecue, funnel cake and cotton candy you can eat. Why don't you and your mom come?"

"It sounds lovely," Neveah hedged, "but, um, well, I'm not sure—"

"Come on. It'll be fun." A flash of wry humor lit his eyes. "And you might get a kick out of watching the members of Team Mayne get their asses handed to them by some NBA players."

Neveah blinked. "How so?"

"Five years ago, our streetball games turned into an annual tradition with me, my brothers and a few of our cousins teaming up against some of our friends who play for the Houston Rockets." He chuckled, rubbing his trim goatee. "We all say we're playing for charity—which we are—but it gets pretty rough and tumble out there on the court. We're very competitive, so no one wants to be embarrassed in front of a big crowd."

"I bet." Neveah smiled. "It sounds quite entertaining."

"Oh, it is, believe me. So why don't you come?"

Neveah bit her lower lip, wavering with indecision. She was nervous about seeing his family again after all these years. Did they know why she'd broken up with Xavier and fled to another country? Did they blame her? Resent her? How would she be received if she showed up tomorrow?

On the other hand, she reasoned, the picnic *did* sound like a lot of fun. And she couldn't deny an overwhelming curiosity to check out the community center she'd read so much about.

She also couldn't deny an insanely foolish desire to spend more time with Xavier. And that, ultimately, overrode any other misgivings she had.

"Come on, girl," he cajoled silkily. "You know you want to."

She shot him a narrow look. "Are you going to make me wait for the tow truck if I refuse?"

A shadow of a smile touched his mouth. "Yeah. I will."

Their eyes held.

After another moment Neveah heaved a deep, exaggerated sigh. "In that case, I guess Mama and I have no choice but to show up."

"Nope. No choice at all." Xavier winked at her, then went to work on the locked door. Seconds after he'd inserted the metal piece between the window and the weather stripping, the lock popped right open. *"Voilà."*

Neveah couldn't help grinning at him. "Still got your touch, I see."

"Of course." After retrieving her keys from the back of the van, he returned to the driver's side and opened the door for her with a gallant flourish. "Your chariot awaits."

Neveah smiled as she climbed behind the wheel. No matter how rough around the edges he'd been—and despite any other faults he'd possessed—Xavier had always opened doors and pulled out chairs for her, melting her with his chivalry and irresistible charm.

Unfortunately, *that* hadn't changed.

Resting his elbows on the open window, he smiled lazily at her. "So I'll see you and your mama tomorrow, right?"

She nodded, letting her eyes roam across his wickedly handsome face, which was familiar but not.

"You know how to find your way back to Houston?" Something else he'd always done—fretted over her poor sense of direction.

She smiled wryly. "I'll figure it out."

"Nah, that's not good enough. Take down my number so you can call me if you get lost."

"I won't get—"

"Pull out your cell phone and program my number, woman."

Rolling her eyes in exasperation, Neveah did as he'd told her. "Happy now?"

"Getting there," he murmured. And she knew that he wasn't referring to her saving his phone number.

She swallowed drily. "Well...I should go."

He nodded, then reached over and brushed his knuckles across her cheek. The gesture was so tender that tears stung her eyes.

A soft, crooked smile curved his mouth. "Enjoy the rest of your Sunday...Heaven."

Her heart contracted at the achingly familiar nickname. "See you tomorrow," she whispered.

Nodding slowly, he straightened from the window and stepped back, then lifted his hand in a small wave.

And Neveah drove away from the ranch, her eyes glazed with tears and her heart more conflicted than ever about the dark past that haunted her…and the uncertain future that awaited.

Chapter 7

It was after 10:00 p.m. by the time Xavier returned home from having Sunday dinner with his family at his mother's lavish estate in Sugar Land. He almost hadn't gone. He'd wanted to spend the evening in peaceful solitude, savoring the memory of Neveah's visit to the ranch. But Birdie Mayne wouldn't hear of him skipping out on dinner. Ever since Warrick relocated his company's headquarters to Houston and Yolanda was released from prison, Birdie had turned every other Sunday into an occasion to celebrate having the family together again. Attendance was not optional.

After parking his Dodge Durango in the detached carport, Xavier made his way across the moon-dappled front yard, his thoughts inexorably returning to Neveah. After he bought the ranch and moved into the house, he'd often fantasized about having her there with him, sharing the home as his wife. He'd imagined them making love in every corner of the house, going for long romantic walks and cuddling on the porch swing after dinner to talk and watch the sun set. He'd imagined their children laughing and frolicking in the lake, tussling with the family dog, playing hide-and-seek and chasing one another across the vast, rolling fields.

The fantasies were so vivid that they'd kept him awake many nights, filled with a restless ache of longing for what could never be.

But little did he know what fate had in store for him.

Little did he know that after all these years, he would be given a second chance to reclaim the one and only woman he'd ever loved.

It seemed too good to be true, Xavier mused as he climbed onto the porch and stood at the wooden railing. Neveah had been gone for so long, he'd all but resigned himself to spending the rest of his life without her. It was an unbearably bleak outlook, but then, he'd never had any reason to believe that a fairy-tale ending was in the cards for him.

His childhood had been anything but a fairy tale, unless growing up in a poor, crime-ridden neighborhood qualified. As if surviving on food stamps and dodging gang violence weren't challenging enough, Xavier and his family had been forced to endure the most insidious hardship of all: Tariq Mayne's drug addiction.

As the painful memories suddenly assailed him, Xavier bowed his head under the weight of them and closed his eyes.

As if it were yesterday, he remembered the day his father's demons had nearly become his own.

The day that changed his life forever.

He was six years old, home sick with the flu. He'd awakened from a nap and wandered out of the small bedroom he shared with his two brothers, who'd both been sent to school despite their protestations that they'd caught what Xavier had. His sister, Yasmin, was also gone, while two-year-old Yolanda was at day care.

As Xavier shuffled down the narrow hallway, he wrinkled his nose at the burnt, sickly-sweet odor that clung to the air. When he reached the living room, he saw his father sitting on the floor, his back propped up against the worn sofa as he took a long drag on a glass pipe and slowly closed his eyes.

Xavier stood still, quietly observing this ritual of his father's that he knew was wrong, even if he didn't completely understand why.

Sensing his presence, Tariq Mayne opened glassy, bloodshot eyes and peered at his son. "Who's that?" he rasped out. "That you, Xay?"

"Yes," he answered in a small voice.

"What you doing home from school, boy?"

"I'm...sick."

"Sick, huh?" Tariq grunted. "You don't look sick to me."

Xavier swallowed, saying nothing.

His father lifted a bony hand and motioned him over. "Come here. I got something that'll make you feel better."

A whisper of unease ran through Xavier, keeping him rooted to the spot. "Where's Ma?"

"Dunno. At work, I guess." Tariq shrugged, as though his wife's whereabouts were of no concern to him. He frowned at Xavier. "Didn't I tell you to come here, boy?"

Xavier hesitated another moment, then reluctantly trudged across the room to reach his father's side.

"That's better," Tariq said, angling his head back to smile weakly at his son. "You don't have to be afraid of me. I ain't no stranger. I'm your daddy. See? You look just like me—you and Zeke. Not like that other one," he grumbled, his expression darkening.

Xavier frowned quizzically. "You mean Warrick?"

Tariq grunted, waving a dismissive hand. "Sit down, Xay. You getting so tall already, I'm getting a crook in my neck from looking up at you."

Xavier dutifully sat on the floor, eyeing the glass pipe in his father's hand with unconcealed curiosity.

Following the direction of his stare, Tariq smiled slyly. "You wanna try some of this?"

Xavier shook his head quickly.

"Yes, you do," his father said knowingly. "I can see it in your eyes, boy."

Dropping his guilty gaze to his lap, Xavier mumbled, "Ma says—"

"She don't have to know," Tariq interrupted. "It'll be our little secret."

After several long moments, Xavier gulped hard and lifted his eyes to his father's face again.

"We all have secrets, son." Tariq smirked. "Even your mama."

His young mind didn't comprehend the bitter irony that laced his father's words. When Tariq held out the glass pipe to him, he hesitated for only a moment before leaning forward. As his father smiled encouragingly at him, he wrapped his mouth around the end of the tube and sucked in a deep breath, imitating what he'd seen Tariq do just minutes ago.

As the potent vapors from the pipe filled his lungs, Xavier coughed and choked.

His father cackled. "There you go, son. That's how you do it. You're gonna be a pro...just like your old man."

Xavier said nothing as a strange buzzing sensation suffused his brain and quickened his heartbeat.

As though from a great distance, he heard the jangle of keys outside the front door.

"Shit," Tariq mumbled, waving feebly at the smoky air.

Birdie Mayne stepped through the door, her arms laden with brown paper bags as she called out wearily, "Tariq, could you come help me with—"

That was when she saw them.

Father and son, sharing a crack pipe.

She opened her mouth and let out an anguished, bloodcurdling wail.

And then she dropped her grocery bags and rushed across the room, kneeling quickly at Xavier's side and gathering him into her arms. "Xay?" she cried out frantically. "Baby, can you hear me? Are you okay?"

He could only stare up at her dazedly.

"What have you done?" she screamed hysterically at her husband. "Goddamn you, what have you done to my baby?"

A week later, Tariq Mayne moved out of the apartment and never returned.

But the horror of that experience had haunted Xavier for years, always lurking in the dark recesses of his psyche. He'd blamed himself for his father's departure, rationalizing that Tariq wouldn't have abandoned the family if he hadn't been caught getting high with Xavier—therefore *he* was indirectly responsible. He'd internalized the guilt, carrying around his secret shame not unlike a child who's been molested. As he grew older, he'd channeled his turbulent emotions into the most self-destructive behavior. He became wildly promiscuous, bedding any and every female he wanted. He'd partied hard, binge drinking with his friends and staying out all hours of the night. He'd hot-wired old cars in his neighborhood and went on joyrides, returning the vehicles before the owners ever suspected they were missing. He'd even dabbled in selling drugs, though he'd never used them, scarred by the memory of what he'd experienced as a child.

In his desperate quest to outrun the legacy of his father, he'd become as damaged and full of self-loathing as Tariq Mayne had been.

And then he had met Neveah.

And she'd turned his world upside down.

She was his angel, bringing heaven to the hell on earth that had been his existence. He'd never met anyone like her. She'd fascinated him with her talk of ancient civilizations, West African ancestors and interpretations of dreams. They'd conversed for hours on end about anything and everything. And when inspiration struck her—sometimes in the middle of a conversation they were having—Xavier would watch contentedly as she sketched out a drawing, losing herself to the whims of her muse. Because he could never stay serious long enough to pose for her, she'd drawn him from memory. When she had shyly showed him the portrait, he'd been stunned by how flawlessly she'd captured his likeness.

He'd always known what an extraordinary gift she possessed. But when she had headed off to art school, he'd felt out of place in her new world, surrounded by artists, professors and scholars who'd lauded her as a young Rembrandt. Xavier, in comparison, had looked like a colossal failure—a college dropout whose only claim to fame was throwing the coolest parties in town.

Taunted by a malevolent inner voice that told him he wasn't good enough for Neveah, he'd started skipping out on her art exhibits and hanging out more with his troublemaking friends. And he'd done a number of other things he wasn't proud of, things he would probably regret for the rest of his life.

Rousing himself from the painful memories, Xavier lifted his head and stared out into the night. Almost at once, his mind flashed on an image of Neveah's soft, dreamy expression as he'd rocked her gently on the porch swing that afternoon.

And he smiled.

He may not deserve a fairy-tale ending with her, but nothing short of fire-breathing dragons would stop him from trying to claim it anyway.

Chapter 8

That evening, Neveah and Delores dined at an upscale Caribbean restaurant located downtown. Over steaming plates of jerk chicken, curried goat and green bananas, Neveah told her mother everything that had happened over the past twenty-four hours.

When she'd finished speaking, Delores said gently, "You had to know that once Xavier found out you were back home, he'd make his way to you."

"Not necessarily. It's been thirteen years. I assumed he'd be married with children by now." Even as the words left Neveah's mouth, pain knifed through her heart at the thought of Xavier starting a family with another woman.

"What I don't understand is why Jordan went along with his little scheme," she continued. "She knows my history with him. Why on earth would she agree to set me up like that?"

"Maybe she thinks it's time for you to forgive him," Delores suggested quietly.

Neveah stared at her. "Is that what *you* think?"

"It doesn't matter what I think. This is your life. I can't live it for you."

Neveah swallowed tightly at the reminder of her mother's cancer diagnosis. Delores was facing the grim reality of her mortality. There was no guarantee she would survive to continue leading her own life, let alone Neveah's.

"At some point or another," Delores said sagely, "we all have to make hard decisions. Maybe it's time for you to let go of the past and give yourself a chance to be happy, Neveah. *Truly* happy, once and for all."

Lying awake in bed that night, Neveah found herself reflecting on her visit to Xavier's ranch that afternoon. She couldn't help but appreciate the irony of locking her keys in the van when, eighteen years ago, losing her car keys had brought Xavier into her life.

She smiled quietly in the dark bedroom, awash with bittersweet memories of the day they first met.

It was a Saturday afternoon. She was sixteen years old, and the proud new recipient of a driver's license. After days of pleading her case, she'd finally persuaded her mother to allow her to borrow the car. As she drove herself to the mall that day, she felt like such a mature, responsible adult. But her euphoria was shattered when, at the end of her shopping excursion, she couldn't find her set of car keys. Panic-stricken, she rushed back into the mall and retraced her steps to every store she'd patronized, scouring the floors and dressing rooms with the help of employees and sympathetic customers. But after an hour of fruitless searching, she trudged back to the parking lot to dismally weigh her options, dreading what her mother's reaction would be. She'd not only entrusted Neveah with her car, she'd also instructed her to be back by a certain time so they wouldn't be late to a cousin's wedding.

Neveah was leaning against the Volvo, fighting back tears

as she tried to work up the courage to call her mother on the pay phone, when another car pulled up behind her. As the tinted driver's-side window rolled down, the bass-thumping sounds of Dr. Dre's summertime hit "Nuthin' But a 'G' Thang" poured out of the stereo.

But it was the driver who had Neveah staring in surprise. Lounging behind the wheel, his eyes shaded by a pair of dark sunglasses, was the most popular boy at Jack Yates Senior High School.

Xavier Mayne, star of the school's basketball team and resident bad boy.

Lowering the volume on his stereo, he called out to her, "Wassup, shawty? Everything all right?"

Hastily dashing a tear from the corner of her eye, Neveah called back, "I lost my keys."

"Damn," he commiserated, shaking his head. "That's messed up."

"Tell me about it," Neveah mumbled miserably.

He studied her for a moment, then glanced down at his watch and frowned, as if he were torn between getting somewhere on time and rescuing a damsel in distress.

The chivalrous instinct won. "I could give you a ride home," he offered.

Neveah eyed him dubiously. Not only was he a senior, but he had a reputation for smooth-talking girls out of their panties and leaving them brokenhearted. There was no telling what her mother would say if Neveah arrived home with him, and she was already in enough hot water as it was.

She shook her head. "No, thanks. But I appreciate the offer."

Fully expecting Xavier to wish her luck and drive off, she was surprised when he lingered to ask, "What're you gonna do?"

"Call my mom, I guess." She gulped hard at the thought,

her eyes pricking with the threat of more tears. Please, God, *she silently prayed,* don't let me make a fool of myself by bawling like a baby in front of Xavier Mayne, of all people.

He nodded at the Volvo. "That your ride?"

"No. It's my mom's."

"So she's gonna have to call someone to come get you, right?"

Neveah nodded miserably. She knew she and her mother would never make it to the wedding on time if she had to wait around for a tow truck to arrive.

Xavier eyed her sympathetically for another moment, checked his watch again, then glanced back at her. "I can get you home, shawty."

"Thanks, but—"

"Hold up. Let me park real quick."

She frowned, watching as he swung into an empty space along the next row. As he climbed out of his car and walked around to open the trunk, she dug inside her handbag for a stick of peppermint gum and quickly crammed it into her mouth.

As Xavier sauntered toward her, she couldn't help admiring the way his broad shoulders tapered down to his slim hips and long legs. He wore Timberland boots, baggy designer jeans and a white wife beater that molded the defined muscles of his chest and showed off thick biceps. A toothpick dangled from a corner of his mouth, adding to the air of lazy insolence that characterized his personality.

He stopped before her.

And her mind went blank.

Prior to that day, the closest she'd ever gotten to him was during the rare occasions when they'd passed each other in the halls. Whether he was alone or rolling deep with his posse, he'd always looked right through her—if he looked her way at all. But that was okay. Unlike most of her female peers,

Neveah wasn't harboring a secret crush on Xavier. Frankly, roughnecks weren't her type, especially when their thuggish behavior frequently landed them in the principal's office.

She preferred more sensitive, intellectual types. Deep thinkers who didn't resolve disputes with their fists. So Xavier's whole rebel-without-a-cause persona didn't really work for her.

But now, seeing him up close and personal... Whoa.

When he turned his head to glance around the parking lot, the diamond stud in his right ear twinkled in the sunlight. But it wasn't his jewelry that had her bedazzled. It was the combination of his smooth caramel skin, melting dark eyes, sexy goatee and full lips that left her reeling. And his ripped biceps didn't hurt, either.

She didn't realize he'd asked her a question until he waved a hand in front of her face. "Yo, shawty? You still there?"

Neveah blushed, embarrassed because he'd caught her ogling him. "I—I'm sorry," she stammered. "Um, what did you say?"

He chuckled, and her face flushed so hard it actually hurt this time. Belatedly she noticed that he was carrying a long metal bar, similar to one she'd seen a neighbor use on his car after locking the keys inside.

Before she could remind Xavier that she'd actually lost her keys, he slid the toothpick from between his lips and pointed it at her, eyes narrowed thoughtfully. "You go to Yates, right? Sophomore?"

Surprised, Neveah nodded quickly. While she'd always known who he was, she didn't realize he was even aware of her existence, let alone that he knew what grade she was in.

"Yeah, yeah," he said almost to himself. "You're the painter. You win all those art contests and shit—I mean stuff,"

he smoothly amended, although she'd heard him use far worse language at school.

"What's your name again?" *he asked.*

"Neveah."

He snapped his fingers. "Yeah, that's right. I knew it was something weird like that."

"Excuse me?" *she said, bristling with attitude.*

"Different," *he corrected, flashing a crooked grin that melted her from the inside out.* "I meant to say it's different."

She smiled weakly. "That's better."

"Nuh-vay-ah," *he repeated experimentally, rolling her name around his tongue.* "What's that, like, heaven spelled backward?"

She nodded reluctantly. "Except it's spelled N-E-V-E-A-H, because the nurse messed it up on my birth certificate." *She grimaced, waiting for the inevitable barrage of jokes that she'd been subjected to her entire life.*

But Xavier merely smiled. "Neveah. Heaven. I like that."

She beamed at him.

He flicked away the toothpick, then thrust his hand out. "Name's Xavier. But everyone just calls me Xay."

"I know," *she said shyly, shaking his hand.* "I've seen you around school."

He smiled. "And I've seen you."

She blushed with pleasure.

He had a way of checking her out without being too obvious, head cocked slightly at an angle, thick eyelashes shielding his eyes as he looked her over from head to toe.

It made her weak in the knees.

Trying to play it off, she pointed to the metal bar in his hand. "What're you gonna do with that?"

"Open your car door."

"Okaaay," Neveah said, drawing out the word slowly. "But I still need a key to get the car started."

"Actually, you don't."

She frowned in confusion. "Then how…?"

His lips twitched, as though he were amused by her naïveté.

As comprehension dawned, her eyes widened. "Are you planning to hot-wire my mom's car?"

"It's up to you," he said, glancing around the parking lot to make sure no one had overheard her shocked exclamation. "Either way, you're gonna have to tell your moms that you lost the keys. At least if I get the car started for you, you can drive home and save her the hassle of having to call a tow truck. Know what I'm saying?"

Neveah nodded, because his logic made perfect sense. Still, she knew her mother wouldn't be thrilled to know that her Volvo had been hot-wired by some teenage rascal. And she definitely wouldn't appreciate having to shell out money to have the car repaired as a result of any damages Xavier might cause.

But Neveah didn't have any other choice. Waiting around for assistance would take too long.

"Okay," she acquiesced.

As Xavier went to work jimmying the lock and getting the car started, she turned away from him, muttering, "I don't even want to know where you learned how to do that."

He responded with a muffled laugh.

In no time at all, he had the engine revved and ready to go.

"Oh my God!" Overcome with relief, Neveah threw her arms around his neck and hugged him tightly. "Thank you so much. I don't know what I would have done if you hadn't come along!"

He chuckled. "It's all good, shawty."

"Seriously," she said, her body tingling with awareness as she drew away from him. "If there's ever anything I can do for you, Xavier, just let me know. Anything."

He grinned crookedly. "Since you're an honors student, can you put in a good word with the principal for me?"

"Um...yeah. Sure."

They both laughed.

"Well, you'd better get going while the car's still got some juice," Xavier advised. "And make sure you don't stop anywhere. Go straight home."

She gave a mock salute. "Yes, sir."

As she climbed into the waiting car, he surprised her by saying, "One more thing." When she glanced up inquiringly, he said, "Go out with me."

She stared at him, convinced she'd heard wrong. "Are you asking me out on a date?"

He chuckled at her incredulous tone. "Is that so crazy?"

"No! I just...I just wasn't expecting it, that's all."

"You got a boyfriend?"

She shook her head quickly.

"Good." He winked at her. "What do you like to do, Heaven?"

She smiled shyly. "I like going to museums, book readings, art exhibits. Stuff like that."

He smiled indulgently. "Then that's what we'll do. Stuff like that."

That first date had turned into many more, evolving into a relationship that lasted almost six years. From the very beginning, Xavier had been everything Neveah could have ever wanted in a boyfriend. He was charming, attentive, adventurous, fiercely protective over her, and smarter than his teachers gave him credit for. He and Neveah were inseparable, spending every moment they could with each other.

But everything had changed when she began attending

a prestigious art college in Austin. Because the school was nearly three hours away, she'd known that a long-distance relationship would take some getting used to. But she'd assumed—and hoped—that she and Xavier could make it work if they both tried. Unfortunately, *she'd* done more trying than he had. She'd returned home practically every weekend to see him and attend his basketball games, which were organized by the amateur league he'd joined after losing his athletic scholarship and dropping out of college.

But before long, she'd realized that the support she was giving him was not being reciprocated. Xavier, who'd always been an ardent admirer of her paintings, suddenly seemed apathetic about her artistic ambitions. He'd stopped taking an interest in what she was working on and blew off her art exhibits. Despite her mother's faithful attendance, Xavier's disappearing acts had left Neveah feeling alone and dejected after each showing. To add insult to injury, she'd started receiving harassing phone calls from different women who claimed they were sleeping with Xavier, providing dates, times and lurid details. Although he'd vehemently denied every accusation, the doubts and fears had nagged at Neveah's conscience, making it hard for her to completely trust him.

And then the unthinkable happened.

Just days after graduating from college, she'd discovered that she was pregnant. She'd been scared yet elated, because she loved Xavier wholeheartedly and wanted to spend the rest of her life with him, even if it meant scaling back her dreams of traveling the world as a famous artist. Marrying Xavier and starting a family with him meant more to her than anything. But before she could break the news to him that he was going to be a father, she'd received another distressing phone call. This time the mistress claimed to be calling from Xavier's bedroom, where they'd just made love. When Neveah heard his voice in the background, presumably as he emerged from the bathroom, she'd hung up the phone and doubled over, sobbing hysterically.

Although she knew she was in no condition to drive, she'd jumped into her car and headed to Xavier's apartment to confront him. But she'd been driving too fast, her vision was blurred by tears and the roads had been slick from rain—a recipe for disaster. Her car had hydroplaned and smashed into a guardrail. By the time Xavier arrived at the hospital, she'd lost not only their baby, but her will to salvage their rocky relationship. She told him that they'd grown apart and she never wanted to see him again. Then, two weeks later, after she'd healed from her outward injuries, she fled to Africa to begin the long, arduous journey of healing her heart.

Neveah stirred in bed, surfacing from her painful sojourn into the past. She wasn't surprised to find her face damp with tears. She'd shed many over the past thirteen years, mourning the loss of her soul mate and their unborn child. Mourning the death of her dreams.

As devastated as she'd been at the time, she understood how fortunate she was to survive the car accident that had caused her miscarriage. But now that Xavier was back in her life, she knew she couldn't allow history to repeat itself. Because if he hurt her again, the heartbreak she could suffer would surely destroy her this time.

Chapter 9

The Labor Day picnic was in full swing when Neveah and Delores arrived the next afternoon. The sprawling grounds of the property were swarmed with hundreds of people roaming around, conversing with friends and enjoying the day's festivities. In a separate area filled with carnival rides and inflatable games, children squealed with excitement as they raced from one amusement to another. A large stage erected in the main pavilion boasted a state-of-the-art sound system and three jumbo screens so that the live performers would be easily visible from anywhere on the grounds. The current band was covering Bob Marley's "No Woman, No Cry," delighting the picnickers who were lounging nearby on blankets and lawn chairs.

The afternoon was humid, but that was typical. Though they might fuss and complain, no true Houstonian would ever allow something as commonplace as hot, sticky weather to hinder their summertime fun.

"This is quite a picnic," Neveah marveled, taking in the

festive scene as she and her mother approached from the packed parking lot. "And I didn't realize how *huge* this place would be."

Delores smiled. "I guess that's why folks call the community center the crown jewel of the Third Ward."

"Definitely." Neveah surveyed the enormous redbrick facility that anchored two outdoor basketball courts, two tennis courts, an aquatic swimming pool, a baseball field and a large playground. And that was just the outside, she mused. She could only imagine how many more amenities were offered *inside* the building.

"Maybe we can ask Xavier for a tour later," Delores suggested.

"That's a great idea." Neveah smiled at her mother, who looked stylishly casual in a mauve halter top, khaki shorts and flat sandals. "Thanks again for coming with me, Mama."

Delores waved off her gratitude. "You don't have to thank me. I've heard so many wonderful things about the community center, as well as this annual picnic, that I've been meaning to make my way over here. You've given me the perfect excuse to do so."

"Good, but just remember the terms of our agreement. We're leaving right after the game and you are *not* to leave my side at any point while we're here."

Delores chuckled, shaking her head in exasperation. "I still don't understand why a grown woman needs her mother to—"

"I'll be damned," intoned a deep, gravelly voice. "Look who descended from her throne and decided to grace us with her regal presence."

Neveah and Delores glanced around to see a tall, handsome, dark-skinned man with graying temples striding toward them. Recognizing Xavier's uncle, Neveah smiled at the same time that her mother's face broke into a wide, delighted grin.

"Well, well, well," Delores drawled, planting her hands on her hips as Randall Mayne reached them. "If it ain't the devil himself—"

Neveah watched in utter astonishment as Randall caught Delores around the waist, lifted her several inches off the ground and spun her around. "As I live and breathe! It's Queenie MacKay!"

Queenie? Neveah mouthed to herself as her mother's laughter rang out.

Randall set Delores on her feet again and gave her an appreciative once over. "Lord have mercy, woman. You are a sight for sore eyes."

"You mean *old* eyes," Delores teased. If she were a shade lighter, Neveah would have sworn her mother was actually blushing.

Randall laughed. "Still got a mouth on you, I see." He turned his attention to Neveah, wrapping her in a big bear hug before drawing back to tweak her nose. "Look at you. All grown up and even more beautiful than ever. Welcome home, Neveah."

She smiled warmly. "Thank you, Uncle Randall. It's good to see you again. It's been so long, I'd forgotten that you and my mother know each other."

"We sure do," he confirmed, cutting a sideways grin at Delores. "Your mama and I, we go *way* back. Ain't that right, Queenie?"

"That's right." She smiled, explaining to Neveah, "Randall and I met many years ago when I was fresh out of law school, and *he* was a rookie cop who hadn't learned to live and die by the proverbial 'blue code of silence.' He testified on behalf of one of my clients who'd been beaten up by a police officer. Randall's the one who responded to a neighbor's call about a disturbance. If he hadn't arrived and intervened when he did, that poor boy would have died." She looked at Randall, her eyes glowing with admiration. "It took a lot of courage for you to testify against a fellow cop."

Randall grunted, visibly uncomfortable with her words of praise. "Well, it's like you said. I didn't know better."

"Oh, but that's not true," Delores told Neveah. "Turns out Randall Mayne was the genuine article—a man who had the courage of his convictions and wasn't afraid to make enemies. A rebel through and through."

Rubbing the back of his neck, Randall muttered, "I don't know about all that."

"I do." Amused by his obvious discomfiture, Delores added, "You stood up for what was right and earned the respect of your brothers in blue."

"Maybe," Randall reluctantly conceded, then winked at Neveah. "I used to tell your mother that if I ever got kicked off the police force—or found myself tethered to a boulder at the bottom of the Brazos River—she'd never forgive herself for making my life a living hell during the trial."

Delores threw back her head and laughed.

Neveah smiled, touched by the warm camaraderie shared by the two old friends. "So where'd the nickname come from?"

"Queenie?" Randall laughed heartily. "That's what I used to call your mother because of the way she carried herself. Head held high, chin up in the air, shoulders squared. She'd march into the police station and ask to speak to the captain, and when his secretary tried to give Delores the runaround, she'd look down that proud nose of hers—like a queen issuing orders to her subjects—and demand that the captain see her *now*." He grinned, wagging his head fondly at Delores. "You used to have that poor woman quaking in her shoes."

Delores blinked innocently. "I have *no* idea what you're talking about."

With a shout of laughter, Randall pulled her close and

kissed her forehead before saying to Neveah, "Your mother's quite an extraordinary woman. I'm glad you brought her today. We have a lot of catching up to do."

Neveah grinned. "So I see."

Randall and Delores smiled at each other, seeming to forget that Neveah was still standing there until she discreetly cleared her throat, drawing their attention back to her.

"Xavier will be out shortly," Randall told her. "The mayor showed up with some out-of-town guests and cornered Xay into giving them the grand tour of the community center. Mayor Parker takes such personal pride in this facility you would think *she* was the one who'd built it." Randall chuckled. "Anyway, Neveah, my nephew asked me to keep a lookout for you."

She grinned. "So you're the welcome committee, huh?"

"*Part* of the committee." Smiling, Randall nodded over her shoulder. "Here comes the rest."

Neveah turned to watch the approach of Yasmin, Warrick, Zeke and Yolanda Mayne.

Her throat tightened at the sight of the four siblings who'd welcomed her into their family eighteen years ago, becoming the brothers and sisters she'd never had.

As they drew nearer, she felt her chin lifting defensively as she braced herself for a frigid reception—which would be only slightly better than the aloof reception of strangers.

After exchanging greetings and pleasantries with Delores, they turned as a collective body to face Neveah.

She stared at them, and they stared back.

Swallowing nervously, she murmured, "Hey, guys."

And then the most amazing thing happened.

They surrounded her, enveloping her in a fiercely affectionate group hug that made her heart swell with joyous relief and gratitude. They clung together for several poignant moments, laughing and sharing fond greetings.

As they drew apart, Neveah blinked back tears that were mirrored in the eyes of Yasmin and Yolanda. Until that very moment, she hadn't realized how much she'd missed these siblings, hadn't realized just how much this reunion would mean to her. She felt like the character Celie in *The Color Purple,* meeting her long-lost children for the very first time.

Warrick cradled Neveah's cheek in his hand as she congratulated him on his marriage and fatherhood. Yasmin and Yolanda gushed over her Afro while Zeke—another bona fide hottie—teasingly called her Cleopatra Jones.

"I hate to break up this lovefest…"

Everyone turned to find Xavier standing there, his eyes glimmering with amusement as he observed the reunion between Neveah and his siblings.

Neveah's heart thumped hard at the sight of him. He was dressed similarly to his family members in a navy blue T-shirt that bore the community center's name and slogan, but—to her knowledge—only *he* wore a pair of dark jeans that rode wickedly low on his hips and clung to the muscled hardness of his long legs.

"Oh, sweetie, you don't have to *break up* anything," Yasmin told her brother as she grasped his arm.

"That's right," Yolanda added slyly, snagging his other arm and drawing him into their circle. "There's *plenty* of room for one more in this lovefest."

Before Neveah knew what was happening, she and Xavier were pushed together, and the four siblings traded conspiratorial grins as they departed.

As Neveah and Xavier stared at each other, a hot flush that had nothing to do with the humidity heated her skin. "Well," she murmured. "*That* was subtle."

His lips quirked, eyes glinting with humor. "My family doesn't really do subtle."

"Hmm." They were standing so close together that she could feel the heat radiating from his body, could smell a trace of soap that clung to his warm skin. She drew a deep, unsteady breath and moistened her dry lips with the tip of her tongue, not missing the way his eyes tracked the gesture.

"Neveah—"

She would never know what he'd been about to say, because he was suddenly interrupted by a series of wolf whistles from a group of young boys strolling by, openly gawking at Neveah. "Dayuum, Professor X! You the man!"

Xavier frowned, eyeing them menacingly. "You boys staying out of trouble?"

"Yes, sir," came the exaggeratedly innocent responses. "Always."

"Better be." Xavier kept his stern expression in place until the teenagers had moved on. Then he chuckled, shaking his head at Neveah. "Sorry about that."

"No problem." But she stepped back self-consciously.

His gaze raked over her, taking in her colorful ensemble. A yellow tube top, a red gypsy skirt that flared above her knees and a pair of flat brown sandals with crisscross straps that laced up to her calves.

"Dayuum," he murmured appreciatively.

Neveah shot him a look, and he laughed. "Sorry. It seemed appropriate. You look good, girl. Damn good."

Ignoring the way her insides tingled with pleasure, she arched an amused brow at him. "They call you Professor X? As in the telepathic leader of the X-Men? Or Professor X, one of the former members of X-Clan?"

Xavier laughed. "Come on now. You know these young heads don't know anything about old school hip-hop. No, the nickname started because of my first initial, and then eventually it became a reference to the X-Men. All the kids complain that I'm always getting in their heads and keeping one step ahead of them, like I can read their minds."

"Can you?" Neveah teased.

He grinned wryly. "I don't need to. I've been where they are. I know how they think, how they're wired. Anyway, where's your mom? Didn't you bring her?"

"I did. She was here a minute ago." Glancing around, Neveah realized that her mother and Randall must have wandered off while she was preoccupied with Xavier's siblings. "I think she's with your uncle. Apparently they haven't seen each other in eons, so they've got a lot of catching up to do."

Xavier smiled. "Come on. Let's go find her so I can say hello."

"Okay."

As they began walking together, Xavier automatically adjusted his long-legged stride to accommodate hers. Neveah slanted him a small grateful smile and he smiled back, silently acknowledging the old habit.

The reggae band on stage was now performing "Everything's Gonna Be Alright," another Bob Marley classic. Neveah unconsciously hummed along, enjoying the music and the lively atmosphere of the picnic. The appetizing aromas of smoky barbecue, roasted turkey legs, deep-fried corn and sugar-drizzled funnel cake made her mouth water, reminding her that she'd skipped breakfast that morning so that she and her mother wouldn't be late to their pedicure appointment. Not that skipping meals was anything new to her. Whenever she was in the throes of painting, she could go several hours—sometimes even an entire day—without thinking about food.

As if he'd read her mind, Xavier asked, "Have you eaten yet?" When she shook her head, he glanced at his watch and frowned. "It's almost two o'clock. You need to eat something."

"I thought you wanted to find my mom first."

"After you have lunch."

He steered her to a canopy-covered pavilion, where dozens of people sat at picnic tables eating their meals while enjoying the cool breezes from overhead misting fans.

"Why don't you find somewhere to sit," Xavier told Neveah, "and I'll fix you a plate."

Surprised, she said, "Oh, you don't have to do—"

But he'd already walked off, broad shoulders swaying as he strode purposefully toward the linen-draped buffet table. Neveah shook her head after him, even as a smile tugged at the corners of her mouth. She'd forgotten how bossy he could be. And overprotective. And…thoughtful.

She frowned, not wanting to remember the endearing qualities that had made her fall in love with Xavier. It would only get her into trouble.

Even more than she already was.

"You're a lucky gal."

Neveah glanced around, meeting the friendly gaze of an elderly black couple seated at a nearby table. "I'm sorry. Did you say something?"

"I said you're a lucky gal. In the fifty years we've been married—" the woman jerked her thumb at the man beside her "—I don't think he's *ever* fixed me a plate of food."

"I've done other things," her husband grumbled sheepishly.

"Of course you have." She patted his hand and winked at Neveah, who grinned.

"If you're looking for somewhere to sit," the woman invited, "you're more than welcome to join us."

As Neveah walked over to the table and sat down across from the couple, the woman said warmly, "We're Mr. and Mrs.

Blackwell. I'd tell you our first names, but, well, you're not old enough to be addressing us by those anyway. No offense."

Neveah laughed. "None taken. My grandparents used to tell people the same thing."

Mrs. Blackwell beamed with pleasure. "Speaking of grandchildren, ours are around here somewhere, having the time of their lives. They're teenagers," she added before Neveah could ask. "Believe me, we wouldn't leave small children unsupervised. We've just been sitting here and enjoying ourselves, staying out of the heat and people-watching. We saw you and Xavier Mayne walking over here. You make such a nice young couple."

Neveah flushed. "Oh, we're not dating."

"No?" Mrs. Blackwell sounded disappointed. "That's too bad. You look so good together. Even the way you walk beside each other made me think you'd been together for a long time."

"No, ma'am."

"Well, I guess that would explain why we've never seen you at the community center before."

"Do you come here often?" Neveah asked, eager to change the subject.

"Oh, we're here just about every day," Mrs. Blackwell answered. "Right now we're taking beginner swimming classes. We figured it's never too late to learn." She shared a fond smile with her husband before returning her attention to Neveah. "Our grandchildren like to hang out at the center, too. There are plenty of activities for them to do, and someone's always here to help them out with homework or talk them through any problems they're having at school."

Her expression softened. "Honestly, that community center has been a godsend to me and my husband. See, we had to raise our grandchildren because neither of their parents was up to the task. We've done the best we can, but the reality is that young folks nowadays face pressures *we* never dreamed of when we were coming up."

Mr. Blackwell hummed and nodded vigorously in agreement.

His wife chuckled before continuing, "Xavier and Zeke Mayne have had such an amazing influence on our grandsons. You should hear the way they come home talking about 'Professor X said this' or 'Coach Zeke thinks I should try out for that.' Honestly, we've never seen those boys respond so positively to *any* adult. It's really something, I tell you."

Neveah smiled, her heart warming with pride at the woman's revelations. At the same time, she realized that the more she learned about Xavier's unselfish generosity, the harder it was to keep despising him and holding him at arm's length.

"It's no wonder that both Xavier and Zeke have received Citizen of the Year and Mentor of the Year awards," Mrs. Blackwell proudly continued. "And earlier this year, the mayor honored them with the key to the city."

"That's wonderful," Neveah said sincerely. She was surprised that her mother hadn't shared this news with her. But then again, Delores knew how excruciatingly difficult it had been for Neveah to hear *anything* about Xavier over the years.

Mrs. Blackwell smiled at her. "Given the type of man Xavier is, I guess it shouldn't have surprised me that he offered to fix you a plate. But I hope you're not *too* hungry, dear."

Neveah gave her a quizzical look. "Why?"

"Well, the way folks keep stopping him to talk, it might be a while before he makes it to the buffet table."

Neveah glanced over her shoulder, watching as Xavier moved through the crowd, laughing and conversing with different people, shaking hands and responding to the warm greetings that were called out to him.

She smiled quietly before turning back to her friendly companion. "I don't mind waiting for him."

"No," Mrs. Blackwell agreed with an intuitive smile, "I don't suppose you would."

By the time Xavier returned to Neveah, the kind elderly couple had left to track down their grandchildren.

"Sorry about that," Xavier apologized ruefully. "I didn't realize I'd get held up so long. I should have just asked one of the caterers to bring you a plate."

She smiled, accepting a plastic cup filled with sweet tea. "That's okay. You couldn't be rude and not speak to folks. Besides, I made a couple new friends while you were gone."

"Yeah, I saw you talking to the Blackwells. Good people."

"Salt of the earth," Neveah agreed, eyeing the large foam container in his hand. "What'd you get?"

"You'll see. Come on, let's go."

"Where?"

"Someplace more, ah, private."

They headed back toward the main pavilion area, where, miraculously, they found the perfect spot beneath a large oak tree. It was partially secluded, with the nearest picnicker at least twenty yards away.

"I can't believe no one already claimed this," Neveah marveled. "Not only is it in the shade, but we've got a wonderful view of the stage. Why didn't anyone—"

Suddenly an attractive young woman appeared, holding a red-and-white-checkered blanket. Thinking she'd come to reclaim her spot under the tree, Neveah instinctively tensed, bracing for a confrontation. But the woman merely smiled at her before passing the blanket to Xavier.

"Thanks, Lindsey." He winked at her, earning a sassy grin.

After she'd moved off, Neveah gaped at Xavier. "Who was that?"

"My assistant."

"When… How did you—"

"Hold this." He handed her the foam container, then spread the blanket on the grass and motioned for her to sit down. She did, glancing around suspiciously.

"What're you looking for?" Xavier asked, stretching out on the blanket.

"I'm waiting for someone to show up with a picnic basket containing a bottle of wine and cheese," Neveah said drily.

Xavier checked his watch. "Not for another twenty minutes." At Neveah's startled look, he laughed. "I'm kidding. Now eat your food before it gets cold."

After arranging her skirt discreetly over her legs, she settled the container on her lap and opened the lid. Her eyes widened at the amount of food he'd given her.

"You don't really expect me to eat all this by myself, do you?"

He grinned, leaning back on his elbows. "Of course."

"No way. I can't do it, but I refuse to let it go to waste when there are so many starving children in Africa. I know—I saw them firsthand."

"There are starving children right here, too," Xavier pointed out wryly.

"I know. Which is even *more* reason for you to help me eat this food."

He shook his head. "Can't. The game starts in three hours. I don't wanna play on a full stomach. Besides, I already—"

Neveah leaned over and slid a forkful of potato salad into his mouth.

"Mmm." His gaze darkened as she slowly withdrew the fork from between his lips. "On second thought…"

Neveah felt a rush of tingling heat in her belly. Without

thinking she licked the tines of the plastic utensil, watching as his eyes turned smoky with desire.

Okay, so maybe feeding him hadn't *exactly* been the smartest move on her part.

Striving for composure, she picked up a juicy pork rib and took a bite. "Mmm, that's some *good* barbecue."

"I know." Xavier's voice was low, rough. "Can I have a bite?"

She smiled. "Nope."

"Why not? I thought you wanted to share."

"Changed my mind." She ate another bite and groaned. "Man, there's *nothing* in the world like good Texas barbecue. God, I've missed this."

The way Xavier was staring at her, she half expected him to pounce on her and pin her to the blanket, onlookers be damned.

"So you're just gonna sit there and tease me," he grumbled. "That's messed up. I see how you do."

She laughed huskily. "Quit your complaining. You already ate, remember? Besides, I don't want to be blamed if you end up playing like a scrub because your stomach was full."

"A *scrub?*" He snorted. "That won't be happening. Trust me."

Neveah grinned wryly, shaking her head at him. "Just as cocky as ever," she teased, suddenly awash with memories of attending his basketball games in high school. Although he'd regularly led his team in scoring, his rebellious nature had kept him on his coach's bad side. So while he'd possessed the raw talent to be named team captain, his bad attitude and lack of discipline ultimately hindered him from reaching his true potential.

Swallowing a mouthful of potato salad, Neveah asked curiously, "What's your team's record against the NBA players?"

Xavier's cocksure expression faltered. "Uh…one and four," he mumbled.

Neveah grinned. "So you're telling me that over the past five years, you guys have only beaten them *once?*"

He bristled, taking umbrage. "They're professional basketball players. They're *supposed* to beat us. But it's not like we get blown out or anything. All of us grew up playing streetball before we went on to play basketball in either high school or college. So trust me, we definitely make these games competitive."

"Uh-huh." Neveah blithely munched on another rib. "But you still have a losing record. Poor babies."

He grinned at her. "So now you're talking trash, huh?"

She shrugged. "I don't need to talk trash. *I'm* not the one who's gonna get my butt kicked in—" she glanced at her watch "—two hours and forty-seven minutes."

Xavier threw back his head and shouted with laughter.

Neveah grinned, enjoying their playful banter so much that she forgot she wasn't supposed to.

As his laughter subsided, Xavier looked at her, amused challenge glinting in his eyes. "I think this calls for a friendly wager."

"What kind of wager?"

He sat up slowly. "If my team wins the game, you have to agree to paint the mural for the community center."

Neveah didn't miss a beat. "I don't think so."

"Why not?"

"I already gave you my answer on the mural, and it's not going to change over the outcome of some silly bet."

"What's wrong?" Xavier taunted. "Afraid you'd lose?"

She snorted. "Hardly. Don't get me wrong. I know how incredibly talented you guys are. I've seen all of you play. But as you just pointed out, you're competing against professional players, and you have an abysmal one-and-four record against them. So, no, I'm not afraid of losing the bet to you."

"Then what's the problem?"

"Okay, suppose I agree to the bet. What happens if your team loses? What do *I* get?"

He hesitated. "Whatever you want."

Neveah held his gaze. *I want you to leave me alone,* she longed to say. *I want you to stop making my pulse go berserk every time you look at me, smile at me or touch me. I want you to stop being a wonderful, caring man who mentors troubled teens, a man who's adored by his family and an entire community. I want you to give me every damn reason in the book to continue hating you and blaming you for the death of my dreams.*

Watching her intently, Xavier swallowed hard and flexed his jaw. As if he'd intercepted her thoughts and dreaded hearing them voiced aloud.

The silence stretched between them. The noises in the background—the sounds of laughter, childish squeals, animated conversations, even the bass-heavy music—faded to a distant hum as she and Xavier focused on each other.

Finally, unable to take the suspense any longer, he prompted softly, "Tell me what you want, Neveah."

After another hesitation, she said quietly, "If I win the bet, I want you to accept my decision not to paint the mural. You can't keep asking me about it, hoping to change my mind. I have my reasons for refusing, so you have to respect that and move on. Can you do that?"

He held her gaze for a long moment, a muscle working in his jaw. It seemed an eternity passed before he shook his head. "Never mind."

She was surprised. "What do you mean?"

"I don't want you to paint the mural just because you lost a bet to me. I want you to do it because you *want* to, because you believe in the project and you share my vision. *That's* why you've become such a celebrated artist, Neveah. Because even a novice can see that you pour your heart and soul, your passion and dreams, into every single piece you create." He shook his head slowly at her. "I wouldn't want anything less from you."

Neveah stared at him, shaken by the depth of emotion in his words. She opened her mouth to respond, but no sound emerged. He'd rendered her speechless.

Noting her stunned reaction, he smiled crookedly. "But don't think you're getting off the hook that easily. I'm not abandoning the bet, just changing the terms."

She eyed him warily. "How so?"

"I want you to have dinner with me."

"Dinner?" she echoed. "That's all you want?"

"Not even close." He gave her a meaningful glance. "But it's a start."

She swallowed hard.

"And just to show you how determined I am to earn the pleasure of your company," he continued, "I'm not only guaranteeing a win for my team. I'm going a step further and promising that I'll score at least thirty points. Just for you."

"Thirty points?"

He nodded, smiling at her skeptical tone. "It's been a while, but I think I can do it. Especially with the right motivation." Deliberately his gaze roamed across her face, landing on each feature with a featherlight touch that accelerated her heartbeat. Slowly lifting his eyes to hers, he murmured, "So do we have a deal?"

She stared at him for several seconds, then shrugged dismissively, as though she didn't care one way or another. "Sure. Whatever. No offense, but there's *no way* you're scoring thirty points against some NBA players."

Smiling lazily, Xavier stretched out along the blanket, clasped his hands behind his head and murmured, "We'll see about that."

Chapter 10

They spent the next hour enjoying the live music and talking companionably while Neveah finished her meal. She told Xavier about her conversation with the Blackwells, congratulating him on the awards and honors he'd received. He acknowledged her compliments with a modest nod, seeming almost relieved when they were interrupted by a vendor passing out cotton candy. Neveah put up only a token protest when Xavier snagged one for her, pulled off a piece of the fluffy pink confection and fed it to her. As he slowly licked his fingers, they shared a sultry smile.

Across the pavilion, popular hip-hop artist Dirty Southz had taken to the stage to perform a series of smooth tracks and bass-thumping remixes that had the crowd singing and dancing along.

"What's up, H-Town?" the rapper greeted the audience during a song break, sauntering up and down the stage. "I know everybody's having a good time, 'cause one thing our people *love* is some free food."

Hearty laughter swept through the crowd.

"It's good to be back home in Houston. For those who may not know, I grew up in the Third Ward, running the streets with some of you hood rats who're still wearing the same played-out gear." More laughter erupted as he shielded his eyes with his hand and pretended to scan the picnic grounds. "Nah, don't try to hide—I see you!"

He chuckled, waiting until the hilarity had died down before he continued. "All kidding aside, though, I was honored to be invited to perform at this year's picnic. Well, actually, I wasn't *invited*. My man Xay called me up and *told* me what day and time I needed to be here. For real, though. Anybody who knew Xay back in the day knows he ain't no joke. When he says jump…*shee-it*, you don't even ask how high. Just jump!"

Neveah joined in the crowd's laughter as Xavier chuckled. Playfully bumping her shoulder, he teased, "You hear that, woman? You taking notes?"

She punched his arm. "You wish!"

"Seriously though," Dirty Southz continued. "I'm proud of the Mayne brothers for what they're doing in our beloved community. This next song is dedicated to them."

As he launched into his Grammy-winning single, "Boyz from Da Ward," anyone who wasn't already on their feet leaped up with a roar of approval. And by the time he got to the catchy verse about Warrick, Xavier and Zeke, everyone was enthusiastically rapping along. Except Xavier and Neveah, who'd only heard the song for the first time on the radio when she returned home last week.

When the number ended, a wave of appreciative cheers and applause swept over the audience. Grinning broadly, Neveah stole a sidelong glance at Xavier, who looked adorably embarrassed by all the attention. Before she could stop to question the sudden impulse, she leaned over to kiss his cheek.

Unfortunately, he turned his head at the same time.

Their lips brushed.

In that exhilarating instant, a rush of pleasure swept through her, torching her blood. As their eyes locked, every instinct screamed at Neveah to pull back before it was too late. But then Xavier angled his head slightly, molding his mouth to hers. And she closed her eyes, surrendering with a low moan.

His lips were even softer than she'd remembered, lush and unbelievably sensual. His hand came up, cupping the curve of her cheek as he deepened the kiss. He tasted like cotton candy and man, sweet and decadently sinful. She quivered as he traced his tongue over her lips and licked the soft inner flesh, coaxing her to open for him. As he penetrated her mouth, a throbbing heat flooded her loins. Her panties stuck to the damp folds of her sex, causing her to press her thighs together.

His tongue captured hers, tasting and stroking her until she thought she would go up in flames. She hungrily sucked his tongue and he groaned, a husky rumble that shook them both. He whispered her name—an endearment, a prayer, a call to seduction. Her body strained against his, shamelessly heeding the summons.

"Well, well, well. So *this* is where you've been hiding."

With a startled gasp, Neveah sprang away from Xavier. As he swore under his breath, she whipped her head around to see who had interrupted them.

To her everlasting mortification, it was Birdie Mayne.

While Neveah's face burned with embarrassment, Xavier looked only mildly abashed as he glanced up at his mother.

"Hey, Ma," he murmured.

"Hey, yourself," came her droll response as she took in the

intimate tableau with obvious disapproval, reminding Neveah of the time she'd come home early from work and caught them making out on the living room sofa.

"You're just now getting to the picnic?" Xavier asked her.

"Mmm-hmm. And not a minute too soon, apparently."

Xavier unhurriedly rose from the blanket, then helped Neveah to her feet.

"H-hello, Ms. Mayne," she stammered awkwardly.

"Neveah Symon," Birdie greeted her with a cool, narrow smile. "What a surprise to see *you* here."

Bertrice "Birdie" Mayne had not aged a day since the last time Neveah saw her. Her complexion was the color of melted caramel and as smooth as ever. Her features were fine boned and lovely, accentuated by short, layered hair that was styled to perfection. Her slender frame was fashionably attired in a leopard-print halter, white linen slacks and jeweled sandals—an ensemble that was better suited to strutting down a catwalk than sweating it out at a picnic.

She openly returned Neveah's appraisal, running a critical eye over her hair and clothes before she drawled, "You're looking rather…artsy."

Before Neveah could decide whether she'd just been complimented or insulted, Birdie turned her attention to her son. "Your brothers have been looking for you," she said chidingly. "The news stations are here for the scheduled interviews and photo ops, and then it'll be time for the team's pregame warm-ups. Did you forget?"

Xavier looked amused. "No, Ma, I didn't forget."

"Just making sure." She smiled, cradling his cheek in her hand. "Remember how I always had to remind you to wash your uniform and take your sneakers to school on the days you had basketball practice?"

He chuckled. "Yeah, I remember. But I'm not in high school anymore."

"Of course you're not. But you know I'm always gonna look out for you and have your back." This was said with a meaningful sideways glance at Neveah. "Anyway, you'd better get going before Warrick comes looking for you. You know how bossy your brother can be as team captain."

"Don't remind me," Xavier grumbled good-naturedly before his gaze shifted to Neveah. "I'll see you after the game."

She forced a bright smile. "Okay."

He sent her a look under his lashes, a deliberate, smoldering glance that let her know that he fully intended to finish what they'd started. She shivered with anticipation.

"Good luck," she told him, although she had a sinking feeling *she* would need it more than he did.

"Thanks, sweetheart." Before departing, he shot his mother a dark warning glance that only heightened Neveah's sense of dread.

Birdie smiled and waved at him, the picture of maternal benevolence. But as soon as Xavier was gone, her smile vanished faster than chalk beneath the swipe of a brand-new eraser.

"I see you wasted no time tracking down my son," she spat accusingly.

Taken aback, Neveah gaped at her. "I didn't—"

"Don't insult my intelligence, little girl," Birdie hissed. "After the way I just caught you with your tongue down his throat, do you honestly expect me to believe that you have no interest in getting back with Xay?"

Neveah flushed with humiliation. "Believe it or not, Ms. Mayne, I didn't come back home for your son."

"And yet *here* you are, draped all over him like he belongs to you. Well, he doesn't. You gave up that privilege when you took off and left him."

Neveah frowned. "I'm not here to—"

Birdie sneered. "You always *did* think you were too good for him. Just because your mama was a big-shot lawyer and you lived in a nicer neighborhood and you could trace your roots to Africa. You thought you were better than Xay—"

"That's not true," Neveah interjected.

"—just because he was misunderstood at school while *you* were told by everyone how special and gifted you were, how you'd grow up to become a famous artist someday. My son was a novelty to you, something to do to pass the time until you went off to your fancy art school. You pretended to encourage his dreams, but deep down inside you always believed he was just some hood rat who'd never amount to anything."

"That's not true!" Neveah burst out furiously.

Birdie smiled thinly, her eyes gleaming with malice. "You think you're the only one who made it? Well, here's a news flash. You aren't! After you left home, Xay went back to college and got his degree. But he didn't stop there. He earned an MBA from one of the top business schools in the world. You hear that? Not just in the country—in the *world*. He had corporate headhunters and Fortune 500 firms beating down his door to offer him a job. After he started working and saving his money, you know what my smart baby did? He put his MBA to work and started investing. He made a killing and walked away with a fortune long before the stock market crashed. When Warrick came to his brothers about opening the community center and asked Xay to run it, he refused to take a huge salary because he knew he didn't need the money. He's worth millions, Neveah. You hear me? *Millions.*" Birdie's smile sharpened with vicious satisfaction. "Not bad for a roughneck from the projects, don't you think?"

Neveah said nothing, her heart pounding violently as she fought for composure.

Mistaking her silence for shock, Birdie taunted mockingly, "What's wrong? Are you surprised to learn that the hood rat you carelessly tossed away grew up to become somebody? Or maybe you already knew. Maybe that's why you came back after all these years. Now that Xay is rich and successful, you've suddenly decided he's good enough for you."

Neveah glared at Birdie, her voice vibrating with controlled anger as she said, "You have *no* idea what you're talking about."

Birdie smirked. "Oh, I think I do." As she reached up to smooth her impeccably styled hair, the sunlight caught and reflected the car keys in her hand. As intended, Neveah's attention was drawn to a platinum key chain bearing the distinctive Mercedes-Benz logo.

Following the direction of her gaze, Birdie preened as she held up the key. "*This* goes to my latest birthday present from Xay. You'd better believe he and his brothers take *damn* good care of their mama."

"Congratulations." Neveah paused, then couldn't resist adding coolly, "I'm so grateful that I've been blessed with my own money, so I don't have to rely on anyone else to buy expensive toys for me."

Instantly she knew it had been the wrong thing to say, no matter how good it had felt coming out of her mouth.

"You little bitch!" Birdie exploded. "How dare you stand there and talk to me that way, after everything you put my son through!"

Neveah was flabbergasted. "What *I* put *him* through?"

"Yes, what *you* put him through!" Birdie's dark eyes were ablaze with the righteous fury of a mother lioness defending her young. "That boy was absolutely *devastated* when you took off and left him. I honestly worried that he might hurt himself! He cut off the family for weeks, would hardly eat or sleep or take any of our phone calls. He was a wreck without you! But you know what? As painful as that whole experience was, I think your leaving was the best thing that could have ever happened to him. It forced him to grow up and become the man I always knew he would be. It also made him realize that what he had with you was a complete sham. You know what he once told me? He said that if you'd really loved him, you *never* would have left him the way you did. And I agree!"

Tears burned the back of Neveah's throat. "I did love him," she whispered, hoarse with raw emotion. "Whatever else you may think of me, Ms. Mayne, please know that I loved your son more than *anything* in the world."

"And yet you dumped him," Birdie said bitterly. "Walked out of his damn life without a backward glance. Some love."

Neveah shook her head, trembling with pain, anger and grief. "You don't under—"

"Oh, I understand perfectly," Birdie said acidly. "Now that you've returned from your world travels, you think you can just waltz back into his life and pick up where you left off. But you're sadly mistaken if you think I'm going to stand by and let you hurt—"

"Oh, look, there she is!" cooed a woman's voice nearby. "There's grandma!"

Neveah and Birdie glanced around sharply to watch the approach of a young, gorgeous woman balancing a baby on her shapely hip.

Neveah did a double take, stunned to realize that the newcomer was none other than—

"Raina!" Birdie exclaimed, beaming so radiantly that Neveah couldn't believe she was the same snarling, hissing dragon lady she'd just been sparring with.

Birdie rushed over, giving Raina Mayne a big hug and kiss

on the cheek before gushing over her grandson, whose face was concealed beneath a tiny baseball cap. "Look at my little Warrick. Aren't you the handsomest baby boy I've ever seen? Yes, you are! Come to Grandma."

The baby turned away from her, nearly dislodging his cap as he buried his face in Raina's voluptuous bosom.

Rebuffed, Birdie dropped her arms and pouted.

Raina laughed consolingly. "Don't take it personal, Mom. He's just cranky from his nap. I knew he would be. That's why I let him sleep a little longer before we headed out here." Beaming a friendly smile, she walked over to Neveah and hugged her warmly. "Welcome home, Neveah. You look wonderful."

"Thanks. So do *you*." Neveah stared at Raina, shocked by the dramatic transformation she'd undergone over the years. She'd blossomed from a skinny waif with braces into a striking beauty with golden-brown skin, exotic features and curves galore.

"I'm sorry I wasn't here to greet you earlier," Raina apologized, gently patting her son's diapered bottom, "but we all agreed not to have Little War outside in the heat all day. Since my parents have been here for a while, they're going to take him home with them when they leave."

Neveah grinned. "Are you sure about that?" she teased, dubiously eyeing the sturdy, dark-skinned baby who'd burrowed his face into his mother's neck. "He looks pretty comfortable right where he is, so I don't think he's going anywhere."

"Oh, he will. My parents have the magic touch," Raina added, dropping her voice to a conspiratorial whisper so she wouldn't be overheard by Birdie, who stood a few feet away talking into her cell phone.

Neveah chuckled.

Snapping her phone shut, Birdie glanced over at Raina and announced gaily, "I'm heading back to the front to meet some friends I invited to the game. I'll see you there, baby."

"Okay, Mom," Raina called back with a wave. "See you soon."

Without sparing Neveah another glance, Birdie strutted away like a *Vogue* runway model.

As they watched her go, Raina shook her head and chuckled. "I think she looks forward to this annual basketball game even more than the players *and* the charity recipients. She invites everyone she knows, then holds court in her reserved seating area and grants interviews to reporters like she's LeBron James's mama. She loves to brag about being the mother of not one but *three* talented sons who can hold their own against NBA players. Don't get me wrong—she's genuinely proud of them. But she definitely enjoys the perks of being queen for a day."

Neveah laughed, then tsk-tsked Raina. "Is that any way to talk about your mother-in-law?"

Raina grinned sheepishly. "I love Birdie, but she's a trip."

"Tell me about it." Still somewhat shaken from her showdown with the woman, Neveah gave Raina a rueful smile. "Thanks for coming to my rescue. I was about to be torn limb from limb before you arrived."

Raina eyed her sympathetically. "I'm sorry to hear that. I know how confrontational she can be. As Randall likes to say, 'Birdie ain't breathing if Birdie ain't bullying.'"

Neveah slanted her a wry look. "Well, she obviously adores *you*."

Raina snickered. "Oh, yeah, honey. Birdie's been nothing but good to me since Warrick and I got married. She threw me the most amazing bridal shower that my friends are *still* talking about. She and I go shopping and have lunch together every other week. She's always surprising me with thoughtful little gifts and keepsakes. When I refused to stop working while I was pregnant, she would come over after I got home and give me foot rubs until Warrick arrived home." Raina grinned impishly. "Between the two of them, I must confess that I'm spoiled rotten."

Neveah stared at her wonderingly. "How did you get Birdie eating out of the palm of your hand like that?"

Raina sobered, a shadow crossing her face. "Let's just say the Maynes have had some bridges to mend," she said cryptically. "But I'll let Xay tell you about that some other time."

Neveah was intrigued, but before she could probe further, Raina blew out a ragged breath. "Whew, this boy's getting heavy. Can we sit down?"

"Sure."

As they sank down onto the picnic blanket, Raina let out a grateful groan. "That's much better. It feels wonderful in the shade. It's hot enough out here without having this twenty-pound appendage attached to me," she joked, pointing to her son curled against her body.

When Neveah got her first good eyeful of the baby's sleeping face, she breathed, "Oh, Raina, he's beautiful. Look at that gorgeous chocolate skin and those thick eyelashes. He looks *just* like Warrick."

"I know. That's what everyone says. That's why he *had* to be named after his daddy." Raina sighed contentedly. "Is he sleeping?"

Neveah grinned. "Like a rock."

"I figured as much." Raina angled her head to gaze down at her son, her mouth curving in a soft, adoring smile. She gingerly removed his baseball cap, then brushed a hand over his crown of black, curly hair.

As Neveah watched the tender maternal gesture, she felt an all-too-familiar ache unfurl inside her chest and tug painfully at her heart. Swallowing hard, she glanced away quickly and gestured toward the band performing onstage. "I don't know how he can sleep with all this noise," she marveled.

Raina chuckled. "Babies are amazing. They can fall asleep anywhere, anytime."

"I see that." Neveah grinned at Raina. "So…you and Warrick, huh?"

"I know." Raina smiled, a demure blush stealing across her cheekbones. "I can hardly believe it myself sometimes. I mean, I've loved him since I was ten years old, and now he's my husband. My *husband*." She shook her head with an awed expression. "I know it sounds corny, but I never knew it was possible to be so ridiculously happy."

Neveah smiled, feeling a small pang of envy. "I'm happy for you and Warrick," she said sincerely. "I wish I could have been at your wedding. I'm sure it was incredibly romantic."

"It was." Raina smiled reminiscently. "We got married in the garden at his—*our*—estate in New Jersey. It was absolutely beautiful." She chuckled. "I tease my sister about being a copycat because she and her husband also had a garden wedding."

"Reese got married, too?"

"Yep. To Michael Wolf."

Neveah's eyes widened incredulously. "The celebrity chef?"

"That's the one." Raina grinned teasingly. "Don't they have TVs in Africa? That was one of the biggest celebrity weddings of the year."

Neveah chuckled sheepishly. "I haven't watched much television over the past several years, but my mother loves Michael's cooking show. And now that I think about it, I *do* remember her mentioning that he'd gotten married. But she must not have made the connection that his new wife was your sister. Wow, talk about a small world."

"I know." Raina smiled, gently rubbing her son's back. "So how does it feel to be home?"

Neveah hesitated, then admitted, "It feels good. I missed home more than I realized."

"There's no place like home," Raina said quietly.

Neveah sighed. "So true."

After a prolonged silence, Raina ventured carefully, "I know Xay's happy that you're back."

Neveah said nothing, absently tracing a red square on the blanket.

Raina watched her. "I assume that's what you and Birdie had words about."

Neveah nodded slowly. "She blames me...for the breakup."

"Hmm." Raina didn't look or sound surprised. "Well, there's always two sides to every story. Birdie, of all people, should know that."

Neveah met Raina's gaze and wondered, again, about the history of her relationship with the Mayne family.

Another silence lapsed between them.

"So...your being here. At the picnic." Raina hesitated. "That's a good sign, right?"

"I don't know," Neveah confessed, hearing the confused turmoil in her own voice. "I honestly don't know."

Raina studied her for a moment. "I know what it's like to be confronted with a past you've been trying to forget," she said solemnly. "And I also know how impossible it is to keep running."

Neveah swallowed hard.

Raina's expression gentled. "I know how close you and your mother are. But if you ever need another listening ear, mine's always available to you."

"Thanks, Raina." Neveah gave her a soft, tremulous smile. "I'll remember that."

"Good. I expect you to."

Suddenly Raina's gaze was snared by something beyond Neveah's shoulder. Her lips curved, and a hot, possessive gleam entered her eyes.

And then Warrick appeared, exuding testosterone and mucho sex appeal in his basketball jersey, breakaway warm-up pants and an enormous pair of high-top sneakers. He flashed a lazy grin at Neveah, then dropped to his haunches beside his wife and sleeping child.

Neveah discreetly averted her gaze as the couple kissed and murmured affectionate greetings to each other. The next time she glanced at them, Raina had her head tipped back and her eyes closed as Warrick whispered in her ear. Whatever he was saying had her nodding and grinning wickedly.

Drawing away, he winked at her before turning his attention to the sleeping bundle in her arms. His expression softened with the pride and joyous wonder universally known by new fathers. As he gently scooped up his son and gathered him against his broad chest, the groggy baby began to fuss.

Warrick shushed him, commanding in a rough-tender voice, "Don't be such a mama's boy."

"Hey, don't call him that," Raina protested. "You'll give him a complex."

Grinning unabashedly, Warrick stood and sauntered away with their son cradled protectively in his arms.

Rising from the blanket, Raina told Neveah, "I'll be right back. I'm going to see my parents off with the baby, and then I have to help Warrick with his, um, pregame ritual."

Neveah gave her a knowing look. "Pregame ritual, huh? You mean, like, prayer?"

Raina grinned, her eyes sparkling with naughty mischief.

"Let's just say there'll be quite a few exclamations of 'Hallelujah' and 'Lord have mercy' by the time we're done."

And then she slinked off after her husband, leaving Neveah rolling with laughter.

Chapter 11

Yolanda Mayne rolled her eyes in disgust as her brothers and cousins were greeted with wolf whistles and catcalls as they jogged onto the basketball court two hours later. "I'm gonna have to start watching these games with earphones on," she grumbled.

The remark drew a round of laughter from Neveah, Raina, Yasmin and several other spectators seated nearby. As dusk approached, most of the picnickers had flocked to the outdoor sports arena to watch the charity basketball game that had been billed as the highlight of the day's festivities.

Upon overhearing Yolanda's comment, one young woman proclaimed, "Girl, don't blame us for appreciating all that fineness in your family."

"I know that's right," another woman chimed in. "Three brothers and eight cousins—and every last *one* of them is smokin' hot. I'll take 'em all!"

Over the hearty echoes of agreement, Raina cleared her throat loudly. "Excuse me," she interjected, flashing the brilliant diamond ring on her finger, "but *one* of them is already taken."

Everyone laughed.

As a spirited debate ensued over who would claim the remaining male relatives, Raina turned to Neveah and nudged her. "Check out *that* confab down there."

Following the direction of her gaze to the home team's bench, Neveah saw that Warrick and Xavier appeared to be deep in conversation, their heads bent close together.

"They're probably discussing game strategy," Neveah guessed.

"Probably." Raina narrowed her eyes. "I'm trying to read their lips. Okay, I think Xay just told Warrick, 'I want the ball…as much as possible.' Yep, you were right. They're strategizing."

But Neveah had gulped hard. Uh-oh.

As she continued watching the two brothers, Warrick laughed and playfully rubbed the back of Xavier's head, the way he'd done when they were younger. Grinning broadly, Xavier leaned back against his chair, then slowly— deliberately—glanced over his shoulder and looked right at Neveah.

Her pulse leaped.

As she stared back at him, he made the universal gesture for eating, taunting her with a reminder of the dinner date she would owe him if she lost the bet.

She smirked, then responded by directing his attention to the row of NBA ballers lounging on the visiting team's bench.

He merely laughed.

While the NBA players may have been the bigger celebrities, there was no doubt in anyone's mind that the members of Team Mayne were the main attraction. With their tall, broad-shouldered, long-legged bodies glistening with perspiration as they ran up and down the court, the eleven brothers and cousins were walking wet dreams—a smorgasbord of eye candy for every female packed into the stands, many of whom probably had zero interest in the actual outcome of the game. Neveah could almost hear the collective feminine sighs that swept across the crowd every time one of the Maynes scored, or flashed a cocky grin at an opponent, or lifted a jersey to wipe at a sweaty brow, briefly revealing sculpted abs.

The players, to their credit, mostly ignored the whistles and catcalls showered upon them, although everyone had to laugh good-naturedly when one spectator yelled out, "Which one of you wants to be my baby's daddy? I'm taking volunteers!"

When Xavier made both of his free throws during the second quarter, another woman called out coquettishly, "Winner takes all, sexy. Now come take me!"

Xavier grinned and winked at her as more laughter swept through the crowd.

Catching Neveah's sour expression, Raina chuckled and leaned over to murmur, "Don't worry. You'll get used to it. As long as you know he's coming home to *you,* it's all good."

Neveah shrugged, feigning indifference. "Yeah, well, he's not coming home to me, so I could care less how many panties are thrown at him."

"Riiight." Raina grinned knowingly. "By the way, I caught that little exchange you two had before the game started. What was *that* about?"

Neveah hesitated. "We made a bet."

"Oh, really? What kind of bet?"

After Neveah explained the terms of the wager, Raina laughed at her. "Have fun at dinner."

Neveah frowned. "You think I'm going to lose?"

"You betcha!"

As the game progressed, Neveah realized she never should

have agreed to the bet. She should have held her ground and adamantly refused.

By the end of the third quarter, not only did Team Mayne have a comfortable lead, but Xavier had scored twenty points. He was on fire—aggressively rebounding, blocking shots, making layups and draining threes that left his opponents shaking their heads.

After sinking an improbable half-court shot that brought the crowd roaring to its feet, he glanced over at Neveah and held up seven fingers, reminding her that he had to score only seven more points to reach his goal.

She dropped her head into her hands and groaned as Raina rubbed her back consolingly.

But her only consolation—and it wasn't much of one—was that Warrick, not Xavier, made the dramatic game-winning shot that sealed her fate. As the arena erupted into thunderous applause and cheers, the two brothers celebrated with back-slapping hugs and high-fives. Then, wearing the wickedly triumphant grins of coconspirators, they looked toward the stands.

Raina blew her husband a kiss.

Neveah rewarded Xavier with a scowl that made him laugh.

Not only had she lost the bet, but to add insult to injury, she had to sit there and watch as Alyson Kelley sashayed onto center court in a strapless white sundress with her Miss-Houston-2006 sash draped around her voluptuous body. Beaming for the cameras, she presented Xavier with his MVP trophy, then leaned up and kissed him right on the lips, much to the surprised delight of the cheering spectators.

Gritting her teeth, Neveah told herself she didn't care that Xavier was being smooched by a woman who was nearly ten years younger than she was. A woman he'd dated years ago, and had probably hooked up with last night.

But she did care. She'd never *stopped* caring, and that would be her ultimate downfall.

As soon as the presentation ceremony ended, she said her goodbyes and made a beeline for the parking lot. When she ran into her mother earlier, they'd agreed to meet at the car after the game. She hoped Delores wouldn't keep her waiting.

.She'd nearly reached the parking lot when she was stopped by Xavier's deep, lazy drawl. "Yo, shawty. What's the rush?"

She didn't want to smile, but damn it, hearing him call her "shawty" after all these years was simply too irresistible.

Slowly she turned and watched as he sauntered toward her, just as he'd done that fateful day. He'd exchanged his basketball uniform for loose sweatpants and the championship T-shirt that had been presented to members of the winning team.

He stopped before her, smelling like fresh cotton underlaid by sweat and damp skin. Smelling delicious. "I can't believe you were gonna leave without saying goodbye or offering your congratulations."

"Congratulations," she said sulkily.

He chuckled. "Damn, baby. Don't get too excited now."

She sighed heavily. "You're right. I'm not being a very good sport. Your team won, and you played one helluva game. So go ahead and gloat. You've earned the right."

His eyes glimmered with amusement. "I'm not going to gloat."

"No, you should. I doubted you and your team, and I talked a lot of trash. So go ahead. Feed me all the crow you want."

He grinned. "I'd say you're doing a damn good job of feeding yourself."

She shot him a dark glance, and he laughed.

"If it makes you feel any better," he drawled, "I'll probably be sore for days after playing like that. I'm not exactly eighteen anymore."

She sniffed. "It doesn't."

"Doesn't what?"

"Make me feel any better."

He laughed, shaking his head at her. "I'd forgotten what a sore loser you can be."

Not wanting to take any more strolls down memory lane, Neveah began edging toward the parking lot to signal that she was leaving. "Well, thanks for inviting me to the picnic. I had a lot of fun."

"I'm glad to hear that. Why don't you stay for the fireworks? The show should be starting shortly."

"I can't," she said quickly. "I drove my mom to the picnic, and she'll probably be ready to go soon."

"Actually," Xavier countered, "I just ran into your mom. She and Uncle Randall were still together, and honestly, she didn't look like she was in any hurry to leave."

Neveah scowled. It was bad enough that Delores had broken their deal and deserted her for the entire day. Now she was going to force Neveah into hanging around longer than she'd intended.

"Let me call her and, um, see if she's ready." She retrieved her cell phone and speed dialed her mother's number. Delores answered after three rings, her voice tinged with laughter, as if she'd been enjoying some joke before Neveah called. "Hey, Mama. I'm waiting near the parking lot. Are you ready to go yet?"

"Actually, baby, I'm going to stay awhile longer and watch the fireworks. Randall talked me into it."

"Oh." Neveah could feel the heat of Xavier's gaze on her face.

"Why don't you stay, too?" Delores coaxed. "They're supposed to be really spectacular."

"Oh, I don't think so. It's been a long day. I'm kinda beat."

"I understand. Well, Randall offered to drive me home afterward. So you can leave whenever you're ready, and I'll see you when I get back."

"Oh. Okay. Well…see you then."

"Bye, baby."

Neveah slowly put the phone away before meeting Xavier's amused gaze. "Told you," he said. "We Maynes can be *very* persuasive when we want to be."

"Tell me about it," Neveah muttered.

Xavier laughed. "You remind me of some pouting teenager who's been ditched by her best friend at a party after they made a pact not to get separated."

"I'm not pouting." At his skeptical look, she grinned sheepishly. "Okay, maybe I *am* feeling a bit abandoned right now. Who would have thought that my mom and your uncle would spend all day attached at the hip?"

Xavier smiled softly. "They *do* look pretty cozy together."

"I know. It's really something." Neveah's grin turned wry. "And just for the record, my best friend never ditched me at any parties. Jordan *always* had my back."

A veiled look passed over Xavier's face, disappearing so swiftly she might have only imagined it.

"And speaking of Jordan," Neveah said, eyes narrowed accusingly, "how did you get her to help you pull off that little stunt yesterday?"

The latter half of her question was drowned out by a rowdy group of people passing by, chanting Xavier's name and congratulating him on the game. He smiled at them and nodded his thanks before returning his attention to Neveah. "Sorry. What were you saying?"

"Never mind." She glanced at her watch. "Well, I'm going to head ou—"

"Not so fast," Xavier said.

Neveah inwardly groaned. She should have known he wouldn't let her get away without collecting on his payment.

"We need to discuss our dinner plans," he told her.

She sighed. "I'm listening."

"Unfortunately, I have a late meeting tomorrow night, so let's get together on Wednesday. Seven o'clock. My place."

"*Your* place?" she exclaimed.

"That's what I said."

"You want me to go all the way out there?" But she wasn't concerned about the distance. She was thinking about how secluded they would be, without the presence of waiters and other diners to act as a buffer between them. She was thinking about plump, succulent peaches dripping with juice that he slowly licked off her body. And she was thinking about the unbelievably sensual, intoxicating kiss they'd shared earlier.

When she looked into his glittering eyes, she knew that he, too, was remembering the kiss—and probably planning an encore.

She swallowed hard. "I'd rather we meet at a restaurant. It's not like there aren't plenty to choose from."

He shook his head slowly. "No restaurant. My house. I'll pick you up and take you home afterward."

"But—"

"No buts. You lost the bet, remember?"

She scowled. "Yes, but I thought I would *at least* have a say in deciding where we eat dinner."

"Nope. Doesn't work that way."

"Says wh—" Once again Neveah was interrupted, this time by the muffled ringing of his cell phone. He slid it from his pocket, glanced down at the caller ID and made a face.

"Sorry about that. I gotta head back. I bailed on the post-game interviews so I could catch you before you left."

"You shouldn't have done that."

He grinned. "And let you escape without settling our wager? I don't think so."

Before she could react, he took her chin between his thumb and forefinger, tipped her face up and leaned down to brush his lips over hers. It wasn't a kiss meant to seduce, but her nipples hardened and her knees wobbled just the same.

Slowly lifting his head, he smiled into her eyes. "Be ready at six."

She nodded weakly. "Wednesday, right?"

"Yeah." He winked at her. "Hump day."

And while she stood there blushing and quivering at the implication of his wicked pun, he turned and sauntered back toward the sports arena.

Chapter 12

Jordan cringed at the sight of Neveah marching into her office the next afternoon. When Neveah stopped before her desk and folded her arms across her chest, Jordan met her outraged stare with a meek smile. "Uh…hey, girl. I didn't know you were coming in today."

"You *hoped* I wasn't," Neveah corrected.

Jordan visibly gulped. "H-how was your weekend?"

Neveah smiled sweetly. "It was nice. And how was yours? Did you enjoy South Padre Island?"

"Oh, very much. It was so relaxing. The hotel was right on the beach, and the seafood—"

Neveah cut through the small talk. "Why did you lie to me about who bought my painting? You and Xavier set me up!"

"I know." Jordan groaned miserably. "I'm so sorry, Neveah. I really wanted to warn you—"

"Warn me? Why did you agree to help him at all?"

Jordan flushed, her gaze dropping like an anvil onto the

desk. "I…I didn't know how to say no. He was very persistent about wanting to see you again, and I guess I, uh, took pity on him."

Neveah gaped at her. "Are you serious? Since when do *you* take pity on Xavier Mayne? His name's been synonymous with Satan for the past thirteen years!"

"I know," Jordan mumbled, assiduously avoiding her gaze. "But like I said, he was very persistent."

Neveah rolled her eyes in exasperation. "You've known Xavier almost as long as I have. You're supposed to be immune to his powers of persuasion. *One* of us has to be."

Jordan said nothing, her hands trembling slightly as she busied herself with straightening papers on her desk.

"I hope I'm not interrupting anything," spoke a voice from the doorway.

Neveah spun around, her face breaking into a surprised smile when she saw her mother standing there, looking polished and professional in a plum skirt suit and matching suede pumps.

"Hey, Mama! What're you doing here?"

"I took a lunch break and decided to drop by and see how much progress you were making on that storage room." Delores divided an amused glance between her daughter and Jordan. "Not much, obviously."

"Hello, Ms. MacKay," Jordan greeted her with more eagerness than usual, no doubt grateful for the reprieve from Neveah's interrogation. "I *love* that suit you're wearing. Is that Dolce & Gabbana?"

"It is." Delores's lips quirked. "You certainly know your designers, don't you?"

Jordan laughed too loudly.

"Have you already eaten?" Neveah asked her mother. "We can go somewhere if you haven't."

"Not today, baby," Delores demurred, moving from the

doorway. "I have a meeting with the other partners this afternoon, so I'll probably just grab a quick bite on my way back to the office. But I did want to talk to you about something, if there's somewhere we could speak in private."

"You can use my office!" Jordan offered, leaping out of her chair as if it were on fire and hurrying around the desk. "I need to check on Chelsea and the temp I hired to clear out the storage room. I was planning to surprise you tomorrow, Neveah."

"You were?" Neveah's voice softened. "Thanks, Jordan. That was very sweet of you."

"No problem." She met Neveah's gaze, her eyes full of gentle regret. "I figured I owed you for that, um, other thing."

Neveah inclined her head, silently acknowledging the apology.

As Jordan reached the door, Delores said quietly, "My daughter may not think so now, Jordan, but you actually did her a favor by conspiring with Xavier. In fact, I'd venture to say it was the most unselfish thing you've ever done for her."

Jordan hesitated, some unnamed emotion flaring in her eyes before she nodded and quickly left the room.

Neveah and Delores stared after her for several moments, their eyes narrowed speculatively.

"Interesting," Delores murmured.

"What?"

Delores hesitated, then shook her head and turned to Neveah. "Let's sit down and talk. I have something to share with you."

Once they were settled on the silk-upholstered sofa near the window, Neveah smiled at her mother. "I'm sorry I missed you this morning. You were already gone when I woke up."

"I know. It was too late to wake you when I got home last

night, and then I had to head into the office earlier than usual this morning to take care of some things since I'll be on leave for a while."

Neveah nodded. "After your surgery."

"Before then, actually." Delores paused. "Starting tomorrow."

Neveah stared alertly at her. "You're going on leave tomorrow? Why? Has your surgery been pushed up? Is everything okay?"

"Everything's fine," Delores assured her. "In fact, everything's *better* than fine."

Neveah went still, searching her mother's face. Her dark skin seemed more radiant than ever, and her eyes had a glow of happiness that made her look twenty years younger.

"What's going on, Mama?"

"I'm going away for two weeks." Delores hesitated again. "With Randall."

Neveah gasped, her eyes widening incredulously. "You're going away with *Randall?*"

Delores nodded vigorously. "We're taking a trip to Ireland. We're leaving tomorrow morning."

Neveah was thunderstruck. "How did this happen, Mama?"

Delores laughed. "It's the craziest thing! Yesterday at the picnic, we were reminiscing about the past and reminding each other about the different places we'd always wanted to visit. I was telling him how often I'd been to see you in Senegal, as well as other parts of Africa and Europe. But I told him that I'd never been to Ireland, and I jokingly wondered whether the hills are really as green as I've always heard. So Randall said, 'There's only one way to find out.' I didn't think he was serious, but the next thing I knew, he was asking Warrick if we could use his private jet, and then we were making travel arrangements. It was all so spontaneous and…" She trailed off with another laugh, her eyes glittering with an excitement Neveah hadn't seen in years.

She smiled softly, her heart expanding with joy for her mother. No one deserved this getaway more than Delores. "That's wonderful, Mama," Neveah said warmly. "You and Randall are going to have an amazing time."

"I think so, too." Delores grinned. "As long as we don't get into one of our famous arguments. Lord, you should have *seen* the way me and that man used to go at each other. It was something else."

"I'll bet." Neveah stared at her mother, struck by a sudden suspicion. "Mama...there's something I have to ask you."

Delores sighed. "No, baby, we were never lovers."

Neveah hesitated. "But...you wanted to be."

Delores fell silent for so long, Neveah thought she had dismissed the question as too impertinent. But then, finally, she nodded. "We were very attracted to each other. Beneath all the bickering was some serious sexual chemistry. But we never acted on our feelings."

"Why not?" Neveah asked softly.

Her mother's expression had turned remote, reflective. "Because I was engaged to your father. And Randall was dating Clarissa, the woman he eventually married—and divorced. Anyway, after my client's trial ended, we both went our separate ways and lost touch with each other." Her lips curved wryly. "I didn't allow myself to think about him until the day you came home and told me that a boy named Xavier Mayne had hot-wired my car for you. Somehow I knew he must be Randall's son or nephew."

"No wonder you didn't whip my butt that day," Neveah teased. "You were too busy thinking about Randall."

Delores smiled. "That's probably true."

Neveah chuckled. "The first time I ever met Randall, he took one look at me and asked me if I was Delores MacKay's daughter. He could see the family resemblance, but more than that, he told me I carried myself the same way. So I guess that makes me Queenie Junior."

Delores laughed, capturing and squeezing her hand.

Sobering after a few moments, Neveah ventured, "Did Dad ever…know about Randall?"

Delores hesitated, then slowly shook her head. "He didn't. And if you're asking me whether my feelings for Randall interfered with my marriage to your father, I honestly don't know. But that question haunted me for years after the divorce, which is why I never accompanied you to Xavier's family cookouts and parties." She met Neveah's searching gaze. "I didn't *want* to know."

Neveah nodded understandingly. She and her mother sat holding hands, saying nothing for several moments.

Wanting to inject some levity into the conversation, Neveah suddenly wiped her brow in exaggerated relief. "Whew!"

Delores eyed her curiously. "What?"

Neveah grinned. "For a minute there, I was afraid you were going to tell me that I was your secret love child with Randall. With him being Xavier's uncle, that would have meant me and Xavier are…"

She trailed off with a shudder that made her mother burst out laughing.

Chapter 13

"I have a confession to make."

"Uh-oh," Xavier intoned, glancing up from the pile of paperwork he'd been poring through to find his younger brother leaning in the doorway of his office, his dark eyes glittering with mischief. "What you done now, boy?"

Zeke sauntered into the room, looking like Mr. *GQ* with his fresh haircut, impeccably tailored herringbone pants and Gucci loafers. Sprawling lazily in one of the visitor chairs, he confessed with exaggerated humility, "I've sinned in my heart."

Playing along, Xavier leaned back in his chair and hummed a note of encouragement. "Speak your mind, Brother Ezekiel."

Zeke made an anguished expression. "I have looked into the sweet, soulful eyes of an angel, and have been tempted to steal her from heaven."

Xavier rocked from side to side. "S' all right, s' all right."

"I have broken a commandment," Zeke declared, his

voice soaring to a theatrical crescendo as he channeled their charismatic childhood minister, "by coveting that which I shalt not have!"

Laughing now, Xavier thumped on the desk. "Testify, Brother Ezekiel. *Testify!*"

"Oh, but my burden is ever so heavy tonight. For I fear that the covetousness in my heart will bring my brother's *wraaath* upon me!"

The laughter instantly died on Xavier's lips. Leaning forward, he regarded Zeke through narrowed eyes. "Which brother?" he demanded suspiciously.

Zeke's face, so similar to his own, broke into a downright wicked grin. "I've violated one of the ten commandments by coveting my brother's woman."

Xavier glowered at him. "The commandment," he said through gritted teeth, "is thou shalt not covet thy *neighbor's wife*."

Zeke's grin broadened. "Oh, good. So I'm in the clear, then."

Xavier scowled. "What the hell are you talking about, Cain?"

"Well, actually, *you* would be Cain since you're older. I'm Abel."

"And you remember what happened to Abel, right?"

Zeke threw back his head and roared with laughter.

He'd been christened after their grandfather, Ezekiel Mayne, but the running joke in the family was that Zeke had gotten the biblical name because their mother had been cursing and screaming to the heavens when she gave birth to him. But no one—absolutely *no one*—outside the Mayne clan ever called him Ezekiel. The last poor sucker who'd done so had wound up in the emergency room.

Which was where Zeke would be headed soon.

"Are you crazy?" Xavier barked. "Did you really just stroll into my office to tell me you're lusting after Neveah?"

Zeke grinned impenitently. "Of course, I would never use the word *lust* to describe my feelings for your soul mate—"

"Zeke," Xavier growled warningly.

"—but I must admit that she is one *fiiine* woman. I mean, she was always cute and all. But damn, bruh, if I'd known she was gonna turn out like *that*—" he sketched an hourglass with his hands "—I would have given you a run for your money back in high school."

Xavier felt his upper lip curling into a snarl.

"Between the Afro she was rocking and that sexy smile?" Zeke licked his lips and shook his head. "Got me wanting to stop by the video store on my way home to rent a copy of *Coffy* with Pam Grier. *Um-mmm-umph!*"

Xavier's eyes narrowed into dangerous slits. "Are you finished?"

Zeke grinned. "Are you?"

They stared each other down.

Half a second later, Xavier was out of his chair as Zeke broke for the door, laughing uproariously as he ducked around Yasmin, who'd been walking past the office.

"Boys! Boys!" she interceded, assuming her familiar role as referee as she stood between them. "Stop acting like children!"

"That's right," Zeke taunted as he backed away down the corridor. "You'd better listen to big sister."

Xavier jabbed a warning finger at him. "Your ass is mine the next time I see you."

"Gotta catch me first. Later, peeps!" Zeke disappeared into the elevator, leaving a trail of wicked laughter in his wake.

Yasmin clucked her tongue at the remaining combatant. "I swear, Xay, sometimes you two behave worse than your five-year-old niece."

"He started it," Xavier grumbled, then couldn't help chuckling at the pointed look she gave him from behind her designer shades.

Yasmin was the eldest of the Mayne siblings. With her smooth caramel complexion and classic features, she bore such a striking resemblance to their ageless mother that they'd often been mistaken for sisters. But where Birdie was slender and petite—hence her nickname—Yasmin was tall and statuesque, with healthy curves that her worthless ex-husband had never appreciated, constantly nagging her to lose weight. When she'd finally worked up the courage to divorce him, the family had commiserated with her while privately rejoicing over her decision. Everyone knew that Harris Gregory had never deserved Yasmin. Were it not for the sake of their young daughter, Sahara, no one would have shed a tear if they never saw the bastard again.

"What're you doing here?" Xavier asked his sister. "Don't you see it's a ghost town?"

The community center always closed the day after the Labor Day picnic to allow the maintenance crews to break down equipment and clear the grounds of the property. Closing for business was also a way to reward the employees for all their hard work leading up to and during the huge event. Xavier and Zeke—the center's athletic director—were the only two who normally came in to supervise the cleanup efforts or catch up on paperwork.

"I know we're closed." Yasmin served as the center's human-resources director. "I just swung by to pick up some files, and Yolanda called from class and asked me to bring home a textbook she forgot on her desk. What're *you* still doing here? I thought you had a city council meeting tonight."

"I did. It was postponed until next week." Which meant he could have had dinner with Neveah after all, Xavier lamented.

Yasmin nodded, starting to edge past him. "Well, let me grab what I came for and head out—"

"We really missed Sahara yesterday," Xavier remarked, folding his arms across his chest as he leaned on the wall outside his office. "She always enjoys herself at the picnic. Damn shame she couldn't be there."

Yasmin sighed. "I know, and she was disappointed, too. But this year Harris insisted on keeping her for Labor Day weekend so he could take her to *his* family's cookout." At Xavier's sour look, she added defensively, "They had fun. There were no carnival rides or fireworks, but she still enjoyed playing with her other cousins."

"That's good," Xavier murmured, striving for magnanimity. He wasn't going to give Yasmin a hard time for accommodating her ex-husband's last-minute change to the visitation schedule, which he'd clearly done out of spite to deprive Sahara of attending the community center's picnic. Despite the abominable way Harris had treated Yasmin during their marriage, she'd never bad-mouthed him to their child. If anything, she'd gone out of her way to preserve the relationship between father and daughter. But that was typical Yasmin, always the peacekeeper.

She smiled warmly at Xavier. "Oh, sweetie, it was *so* wonderful to see you and Neveah together again. I'm so happy she's back home. We all are. Well, except Ma," she amended grimly. "After the basketball game, she pulled us aside and went on the warpath about Neveah being at the picnic."

Xavier grimaced. "I figured she might."

"You should have seen the way she was glaring daggers into Neveah during the game. Every time you scored and looked over at Neveah, I thought Ma would lose her mind and cause a scene. Thankfully, your woman didn't seem to notice all the haterade." Yasmin grinned slyly. "She only had eyes for you."

Xavier smiled lazily. "Speaking of eyes, I want to see yours when I'm talking to you."

As he reached out, Yasmin jerked away from him. "Xay, don't—"

But he'd already plucked the sunglasses off her face. When his gaze landed on the purplish bruise surrounding her left eye, the haze that smothered his brain was swift, dark and savage.

"What happened to you?" he demanded, cupping her chin in his hand and angling her face toward the overhead lights. "Did someone *hit* you?"

Seeing the leashed violence in his eyes, Yasmin blanched. "It was an accident. We were arguing about Sahara, and we both got heated—"

"Wait a minute." Xavier eyed her incredulously. "*Harris* did this to you?"

Yasmin hesitated, then nodded tightly.

"Son of a bitch!" Xavier exploded, the words reverberating up and down the empty corridor.

Yasmin flinched as he slammed his fist against the wall, crunching the sunglasses he held. "Xay, listen to me," she began tremulously. "Let me just explain what hap—"

"You're not even married to that piece of shit anymore," Xavier roared, "and he's putting his damn *hands* on you?"

Tears shimmered in Yasmin's eyes. "Please don't tell Warrick or Zeke—"

Xavier stared at her, struck by a horrifying new thought. "Has he ever—"

"No! I swear to you, Xay, this is the first time he's ever hit me!"

"It's gonna be the *last* time, too." With fury choking the air from his lungs, Xavier stormed into his office and grabbed his suit jacket and keys from the desk. As he marched back across the room, Yasmin tried one last appeal. "Baby boy, *please* don't go over there. You'll only make matters w—"

Xavier pressed a quick, hard kiss to her forehead and handed back the ruined sunglasses. "I'll buy you another pair. Now go home, and take the day off tomorrow."

"Xay—"

But he'd already stalked off down the corridor, spoiling for blood.

Twenty minutes later, he strode through the glass doors of the downtown investment firm where his former brother-in-law worked. The receptionist glanced up with a friendly smile of recognition that evaporated as soon as she saw the ferocious expression on his face.

"I'm sorry, Mr. Mayne, but we're about to clo—"

"This won't take long," he growled, barely glancing at her as he stalked past her desk and headed toward the back offices.

"Sir, wait!" she sputtered. "You can't go back there!"

Ignoring her shocked protests, Xavier turned a corner and marched through the open doorway of Harris Gregory's office. The bastard was seated behind a large mahogany desk, his chair tipped back as he laughed and talked on the phone.

The receptionist hurried after Xavier. "Mr. Mayne, please—"

He slammed the door on her face, turned the lock and charged across the room. Harris looked up quickly, his eyes widening with alarm when he saw Xavier bearing down on him like a locomotive.

The phone receiver clattered to the desk as he exclaimed, "What the—"

"You goddamn son of a bitch!" Xavier snarled, ramming his fist into Harris's face.

The savage blow sent the man toppling backward in his chair with a howl of agony. But Xavier wasn't finished. Fueled with lethal rage, he reached down and grabbed Harris by the lapels of his suit jacket, hauling him to his feet as the receptionist pounded frantically on the locked door.

"Xay, come on, man," Harris pleaded as blood leaked from his nose and dribbled into his mouth. "It was j-just a misunderstanding—"

Xavier hefted him several inches off the floor and drove him backward, slamming him up against the wall and banging his head. Taking grim satisfaction in Harris's pathetic whimper of pain, Xavier shoved his face into his and snarled, "You sniveling little piece of shit. The only 'misunderstanding' here is the one you had when you lost your damn mind and put your hands on my sister. Give me *one* reason I shouldn't throw you out this window right now."

Trembling violently, Harris gulped hard and squeezed his eyes shut.

Xavier gave him a vicious shake, thumping his head on the wall again. "I'm talking to you!"

Harris let out a strangled groan. *"Come on, Xay—"*

Xavier sneered contemptuously. "Not so big and bad now, huh? You like hitting women, but where's your swagger now? Huh? Damn coward. I never knew what Yasmin saw in your lame ass, but I respected her decision to marry you. We all gave you the benefit of the doubt, which is way more than you ever deserved. As if you didn't put her through enough hell *before* the divorce, now you're *beating* on her? Let me tell you something. The only reason you're still breathing is that you're my niece's father, and I know what the absence of a father—even a lousy one—can do to a child. But if you *ever* lay a hand on my sister again, I'll bury you myself and tell Sahara the devil called you home."

As Xavier released him abruptly, Harris slumped to the floor with a weak groan.

That should have been the end of it.

But as Xavier pivoted on his heel, intending to leave, Harris decided to salvage a scrap of his questionable manhood by rasping out, "I guess it's true what they say… Like father, like son."

Xavier went deadly still.

Harris made a low wheezing sound that could have been laughter. "Yasmin used to tell me how your old man was a crackhead, how he liked getting high and smacking your mother around whenever she complained about his drugs and all his women. Your sister said—" Harris paused to spit out a mouthful of blood "—she said he had a nasty temper, a mean streak that scared the shit out of everyone but you. I guess that's why you turned out the way you did. A sadistic bully. Just like—"

Harris shrank back against the wall as Xavier suddenly rounded on him, his eyes blazing with lethal fury. "Get up so we can finish this—"

The receptionist burst into the office, keys jangling, her voice shrill with panic. "Mr. Mayne, I have to insist that you leave *right now,* or I'll have no choice but to call security!"

Without sparing her a glance, Xavier knelt over Harris's cowering form and seized his bloody face in an iron grip, forcing him to meet his feral gaze. "Listen to me and listen good. You haven't *seen* what a sadistic bully I can be. You got off easy today. But if you ever touch my sister again, I won't be the only one you have to deal with. Next time I'm coming back with my brothers, and after they take turns whaling on your sorry ass, I'm finishing you off. Believe that."

"Sir, please!" the receptionist interjected desperately.

Raking Harris with a look of scathing contempt, Xavier shoved his head back against the wall, then deliberately wiped his blood-smeared palm down the front of the man's Armani suit jacket.

As Harris eyed him blearily, Xavier rose to his feet and stalked out of the office.

Chapter 14

Neveah was waiting for him when he arrived home that evening.

She'd been there for twenty minutes, rocking gently on the porch swing as she enjoyed the soft summer breeze and listened to the tranquil chorus of nocturnal insects. Outwardly she appeared calm and relaxed. Inwardly her stomach was a vicious tangle of nerves, and her thoughts churned as she mentally replayed the frantic phone call she'd received that evening.

Yasmin Mayne had tracked her down at the art gallery. On the verge of hysteria, she'd quickly explained the details of her altercation with her ex-husband, followed by Xavier's enraged reaction when he'd discovered her injury.

"I think he's going to kill him," Yasmin had cried, "and I don't think our family can survive another one of us going to prison!"

Neveah's confusion over this revelation had been outweighed

by her immediate concern for Xavier. "How long ago did he leave?"

"You won't be able to stop him. I've been calling Harris at the office, but he's not answering his extension or his cell phone, and he must have instructed the receptionist to send my calls straight to voice mail. By the time I thought of calling you, it was too late, and then I had to find a way to reach you. I wish I'd gotten your number at the picnic!"

"It's okay," Neveah said soothingly, trying to calm her down. "Tell me what you need me to do."

Yasmin exhaled a long, deep breath that shuddered over the line. "Assuming Xay doesn't get arrested for killing Harris, could you go over to his place and make sure he's okay? He's not answering his phone, either, and I know how he gets when he's really upset about something. He…he goes into a dark place where no one can reach him." Her voice softened imploringly. "Except you, Neveah. You've always been able to reach him."

So here she was, prepared to do an intervention—terrified she'd end up needing one herself.

When she saw the beam of headlights coming down the road, her pulse quickened.

When she saw him climbing out of his truck, her heart lurched into her throat.

Hoping the element of surprise would give her a slight advantage, she'd parked around the side of the house so he wouldn't spot her car from the road.

He wore a dark, brooding expression as he walked across the ranch yard, his suit jacket slung over one shoulder, his briefcase clasped in the other hand. Her stomach turned when she spied the small dark splotches that decorated the front of his shirt. Bloodstains, she assumed, and could only imagine what had transpired between him and Harris Gregory.

Xavier didn't see her at first, so absorbed was he in his

grim musings. He looked lonelier than a conquering warrior returning alone from battle, haunted by the memory of fallen comrades. As Neveah watched him, her heart squeezed painfully in her chest.

As much as she loved him, she'd never been able to rescue him from his demons. It had taken years, and a lot of heartache, for her to accept the fact that she never would.

As he neared the house, he glanced up. His eyes widened in surprise when he saw her rocking quietly on the porch swing. "Neveah?"

She smiled. "About time you showed up. It's almost seven-thirty."

He slowly climbed the porch steps, his eyes latched onto hers. "What're you doing here?"

"What do you mean? I'm here for dinner. You know, to settle our friendly little wager. Remember?"

"I told you Wednesday."

She frowned, pretending to be flummoxed. "Are you sure?"

His lips quirked. "Positive."

She huffed an exasperated breath. "Are you telling me that I got all gussied up and drove all the way out here for *nothing?*"

His dark gaze swept over her, taking in the flirty length of her strapless red dress and stiletto heels that accentuated her shapely calves. The eyes that traveled back up to her face glittered with pure masculine appreciation, along with suspicion.

"What's going on, Neveah?" he murmured.

"I told you—"

"Yasmin called you, didn't she?"

Neveah hesitated, then nodded. "She told me what happened."

As if they were touching, she felt every muscle tense in Xavier's body. He looked at her without speaking.

"She said you headed straight to Harris's office," Neveah continued. "She tried, but she couldn't stop you."

His jaw hardened, and his chin angled in defense as he braced himself for her condemnation. Her heart contracted, a wave of tenderness welling inside her. She marveled that this strong, powerful, virile man could evoke such fiercely protective instincts in her, even after all these years and after everything they'd been through.

"Did you beat him up?" she asked quietly.

"Hardly touched him."

She arched a brow, glancing skeptically at his bloodstained shirt.

His lips twisted cynically. "Let's just say I didn't 'touch' him as much as I would have liked to."

Neveah nodded slowly. "Your sister thought you might kill him."

"Well, I didn't. So she doesn't have to worry."

"She wasn't worried about Harris. She was worried about you." Neveah paused. "And so am I."

She saw a quick flash of grief in his eyes before his expression grew shuttered. "I'm fine," he said gruffly, walking to the front door and unlocking it. "But thanks for your concern."

Deliberately ignoring the fact that she'd just been dismissed, Neveah continued rocking gently on the swing.

"You know," she began conversationally, "the first time I ever saw you in school, you were fighting another boy. I can't recall what it was about. Some turf war, probably. I was a freshman that year, and I remember being naively appalled that high school students still fought like children on a playground."

Xavier's back stiffened, but he didn't turn around.

She smiled ruefully. "I guess being the daughter of a civil rights activist who'd participated in peace marches also made me somewhat sensitive to, ah, black-on-black violence. Anyway, I stood in the cheering crowd that day, watching as you wiped the floor with your opponent and got hauled off to the principal's office. And that's when I decided you were a thug who only knew how to resolve conflicts with his fists."

Xavier spun from the door. "If you think I'm going to apologize for setting Harris straight—"

"But then I met you," Neveah continued, calmly speaking over him. "And the more I got to know you, the more I realized that you were so much more than a brawler who liked flexing muscle just for the hell of it. The more I got to know you, the better I understood just how complex you were, how caring, how…vulnerable. I discovered that some of those fights—not all, but *some*—happened because you were defending other students who couldn't defend themselves. And once we started dating, I couldn't deny that there was a certain appeal to having a man who made me feel safe and protected, a brother who could handle his business if the need ever arose."

Xavier was staring at her, his expression guarded. "What are you saying, Neveah?"

"What I'm saying," she murmured, rising slowly from the swing and walking toward him, "is that one of the things I initially misunderstood about you became the very same quality that made me fall in love with you. I *love* how protective you are, how devoted you are to your family and everyone you care about. So why would I ask you to apologize for coming to your sister's rescue, when it was your chivalry that won my heart all those years ago?"

As her words registered, Xavier's face contorted with raw emotion. Before Neveah could draw her next breath, he dropped his jacket and briefcase, hauled her into his arms and crushed his mouth to hers. She flung her arms around his neck and kissed him back, matching his hungry desperation.

He growled deep in his throat, a primitive sound that electrified her senses. When he lifted her easily into his arms, she didn't hesitate to wrap her legs tightly around his waist. He groaned again, sliding his hands up her short dress and cupping her bottom through her lace underwear. She shivered, the heat of his touch scorching her nerve endings and making her clitoris swell.

"Inside," she breathed against his mouth.

But he was already opening the front door and carrying her across the threshold. A soft, warm glow flooded the foyer, although she hadn't seen him turn on any lights. She heard a loud crash, and dimly realized that he'd swept something to the floor to clear space for her on the console table. As he set her down, she dazedly visualized the exquisite ceramic vase she'd admired during her previous visit to his house.

"Hope that wasn't valuable," she panted.

"Housewarming gift. It can be replaced." Her head fell back as his lips and tongue trailed a simmering pathway of nerves along her neck and collarbone, sucking at the pulse beating at the hollow of her throat until she moaned.

His big hands traced the curves of her body, skimming the underside of her breasts. She quivered, arching backward as he cupped her through her strapless dress. She groaned as his thumbs circled, rubbing slowly, until her nipples hardened almost painfully.

"You're not wearing a bra," he murmured.

"N-no," she stammered breathlessly.

"You've been living in Africa too long, bushwoman," he teased.

Her throaty laughter dissolved into a gasp as he tugged down her dress, releasing her breasts with a soft bounce. She trembled, watching as his eyes hungrily devoured her nudity before his dark head descended to an erect nipple. She cried out as he gave it a light, teasing flick of his wet tongue before his mouth closed over the taut flesh, sending waves of erotic sensation crashing through her. She held his head to her as he tugged on her nipple, licking between each gentle, insistent pull. The pleasure was so intense that tears sprang to her eyes.

"Xavier," she whimpered helplessly. "Please…"

He laved and suckled her other breast before dragging his mouth back up to her throat. "What do you want?" he whispered huskily, his breath hot and tantalizing against her skin. "Tell me and I'll give it to you. Any way you want it, for as long as you can take it."

Neveah groaned, her loins throbbing in wanton response. *Have mercy!*

His lips returned to hers, their mouths opening and closing over each other's as they shared a ravenous kiss. Desperate to touch him, to feel the heat of his skin against the aching tips of her breasts, she tugged his shirttail and undershirt from his waistband as he went to work on the buttons. He groaned as she rubbed her hips against the huge bulge tenting the front of his pants, eager to have him inside her. It had been too damned long.

But suddenly he tore his mouth from hers, his chest heaving as he gasped for breath. "Wait. *Wait.*"

She eyed him frantically. "Why?"

He rested his damp forehead against hers, his muscles quivering as he fought for self-control. "We need to slow down, baby. This isn't quite the way I pictured our first time after—"

She kissed him hard, silencing him. "It's not our first time, and this is *exactly* the way I've pictured us together. Make love to me, damn it, and don't you *dare* handle me like a virgin."

His eyes darkened to smoldering. That was all the encouragement he needed.

Reaching under her dress, he grabbed the waistband of her panties. "Ease up," he commanded roughly.

She arched off the table, and he dragged the scrap of red lace past her hips, down her legs and over her stiletto heels. She stared at him as he buried his nose in her panties and inhaled her scent, his eyes closing with masculine appreciation.

"Just as sweet as I remember," he rumbled huskily.

She shuddered uncontrollably as he pocketed her underwear, then reached between her thighs and cupped her wet, throbbing sex. She moaned loudly, her hips straining against his hand as he strummed her swollen clit before easing one long finger inside her. As her inner muscles contracted around him, he slowly removed his glistening middle finger and slid it into his mouth.

"Mmmm," he crooned, his eyes glittering with fierce arousal. "You *taste* just as sweet, too."

That did it.

Neveah attacked his unbuttoned shirt, ripping it off his shoulders as he tugged his undershirt up and over his head, revealing a wide chest honed with solid muscle. She ran eager hands over him, but there was little time for her to explore and feast. As he unfastened his belt buckle and zipper, she yanked his pants and dark briefs over his taut, powerful thighs. His penis bobbed between them, a thing of pure beauty. Thick, long, bulging with veins and protruding from a nest of short, dark hair. As carnal need cut through Neveah's veins, her sex quivered and pulsed. Dazedly she stared at his erection, wondering whether he'd gotten even bigger than she remembered.

When a pearly drop of pre-cum trickled from the engorged head, she licked her lips and raised her eyes to Xavier's. He was watching her from beneath his lashes, nostrils flared, his face hard and dark with barely restrained lust. Their gazes locked as she wrapped her fingers around his granite-smooth girth and stroked him sensually, wrenching an agonized groan from his throat.

His hands shook as he retrieved a condom from his pants pocket, tore the packet open with his teeth and sheathed himself with practiced ease.

"Bedroom," he rasped, lifting her off the table and staggering a few steps. That was as far as he got before he gave up, backing her against the nearest wall instead. She tightened her thighs around him and gripped his muscular shoulders, trembling with anticipation and need.

They stared into each other's eyes as he palmed her butt and filled her with one deep, penetrating stroke. As she cried out, he shuddered violently and closed his eyes in an expression of such unadulterated ecstasy, she nearly came just from watching him.

As he slowly reopened his eyes, she shivered from the searing intensity of his gaze. "Heaven," he whispered reverently. "You don't know how long I've dreamed of making love to you again. I've missed you, baby. *Missed you so damn much*."

Her heart swelled to aching. "I've missed you, too," she confessed huskily.

Tender gratitude softened his features. "That's because we belong together."

Even in the heat of passion, with every inch of her body already enslaved to him, some tiny part of her still resisted his claim. "Xavier—"

"We do." His dark, possessive gaze blazed into hers. "And I'm gonna prove it to you. Right here, right now."

She cried out hoarsely as he drew back and thrust into her again, burying himself deeper, stretching her with his thick, throbbing fullness. She moaned and clung to him as he began pumping into her, moving her up and down the wall with the force of each deep, relentless stroke. He demanded her total surrender and she gave it, helpless to do otherwise.

Suddenly nothing else mattered. Her fears, her grief, her anger and resentment over their tempestuous past. Everything was obliterated in this moment of fierce, consuming passion.

Her nails raked his broad back and dug into the flexing muscles of his firm, round butt. He lowered his head, sucking one of her bouncing breasts into the hot cavern of his mouth. She arched backward, keening with pleasure.

He rocked against her, possessing her with long, savage strokes that sent her heels clattering to the floor. The silence of the house was filled with the symphony of their primitive cries and moans, punctuated with shouts of ecstasy. Every breath she took was ripe with the intoxicating musk of their lovemaking. Her heart thundered furiously as a heavy, delicious pressure flooded her womb.

Within moments she exploded, sobbing Xavier's name as a powerful orgasm tore through her body and stretched her taut against him. He followed seconds later with a fury of pistoning hips, calling out her name like a prayer.

They clung desperately to each other, their sweaty bodies racked with deep spasms and shudders. Overcome with the sweet joy of her release, Neveah buried her face in the damp crook of his neck and wept softly.

He swore under his breath and whispered soothingly to her, brushing tender kisses along her temple. "Was I too rough? Damn it, I knew we should have slowed—"

"It's okay," she assured him. "You weren't too rough at all. You were perfect. *Better* than perfect."

She felt his lips curve against her temple. "That's a good thing, right?"

She let out a teary laugh. "That depends."

"On what?"

"Well, it's just that… To be perfectly honest with you, I'd been hoping that our amazing chemistry was just a product of the raging hormones of two crazy kids in love."

He chuckled softly. "I could have told you that wasn't the case."

She sighed. "I know. But you were my first, so back then, I didn't have any other frame of reference."

He went still. "And…now?"

Hearing the jealous edge to his voice, Neveah grinned. "If you're asking me whether I've been with other men since I left home, the answer is yes. Seriously, Xay. Did you think I've been living like a cloistered nun for the past thirteen years?"

"I wouldn't have minded," he grumbled darkly.

Laughing, she lifted her head from his shoulder and linked her fingers behind his nape. "I don't even know why I'm telling you this—and I'll probably regret it later—but you'll be happy to know that you're *still* the best lover I've ever had. No one else compares."

His gaze softened on her face. "I feel the same about you, Neveah."

Pleasure speared through her veins, melting her insides. As she gazed into his earnest eyes, she decided that tonight—*just for tonight*—she would allow herself to believe whatever he told her.

Smiling coyly, she leaned close and nibbled on his lush lower lip. "Now that I've inflated your ego," she purred, "think you're up for an encore?"

"Up?" he murmured, his eyes glinting wickedly as his thick erection throbbed inside her. "Sweetheart, I never went down."

Chapter 15

He stayed "up" through two more rounds of fevered lovemaking, after which they both collapsed upon his bed in a tangled heap of sweaty limbs. When they'd first entered the enormous bedroom suite, Xavier had strode to the French doors and flung them open to let in a gentle breeze, telling her with a wink, "It's about to get *real* hot up in here."

How right he'd been.

Now, sighing contentedly, Neveah hitched one leg over his strong thighs and snuggled against him. He kissed her forehead and drew her protectively closer. She savored the hard-muscled strength of his arm beneath her neck, the familiar warmth of his body.

For several minutes neither spoke, content to listen to the soothing night sounds and bask in the balmy breeze that wafted through the doors to wash over their damp, sated flesh. Neveah thought she could stay right there for the rest of eternity—a decidedly dangerous thought.

What *hasn't* been dangerous about this night? she mused.

Shoving the unsettling question aside, she murmured, "Do you remember the first time we ever made love?"

"Of course." There was a smile in Xavier's voice. "You made me wait an entire year."

"Damn straight." She grinned. "I was only sixteen when we met. I wasn't giving up the goods until you'd proved that you were serious about me."

"And I totally respected that."

"Yes, you did. I was very proud of you."

His chuckle was a low, husky rumble against her ear. "Well, now, I didn't say it was *easy*."

"I know it wasn't. You had girls throwing themselves at you left and right, and your friends teased you mercilessly about being whipped."

"I was. Most definitely."

Her insides warmed with pleasure. "So was it worth the wait?"

"Hell, yeah," he growled.

"I think so, too." She smiled softly, awash with memories. "What do you remember about that night, Xay?"

"Everything."

Silence.

"Like?" she prompted, because men—no matter how romantic they were—always needed prompting to elaborate.

She felt him smile against her temple. "I remember how nervous we both were. You, because you were a virgin. Me, because I didn't want to disappoint you."

Neveah grinned. "You were so adorable. The way you kept clearing your throat and asking me whether the temperature was okay, if I was too hot or cold. If I didn't know better, I would have thought it was your first time, too."

"It *was* my first time."

She snorted. "Yeah, *riiight*."

He tipped her chin up so that he could look into her eyes.

"It was my first time making love," he said quietly. "Every other time was just meaningless sex."

Neveah held his steady gaze for a moment, then swallowed hard and glanced away. "I remember how delighted I was when I arrived at your off-campus apartment and saw how much thought you'd put into creating a romantic atmosphere. You had soft candlelight, rose petals, my favorite chocolate dessert, Babyface crooning in the background—the works."

"I wanted to make it special for you," Xavier said gently.

"You did," she said sincerely. "It was the most beautiful night of my life."

"Mine, too." His arms went around her, holding her close. She brushed her lips against his throat, inhaling the wonderful musk of his warm skin. They cuddled for a few minutes, each lost in their own memories, some better than others.

"What made you come back?" Xavier asked softly.

Neveah hesitated for a long moment. "My mother has cancer."

"What?"

Slowly she lifted her head from his chest to meet his stunned gaze. "It's uterine cancer."

"Oh, baby." Xavier tenderly cupped her face between his hands. "I'm so sorry."

His gentle compassion made her throat ache. "It was caught early, so her doctors are very optimistic about her prognosis. So optimistic, in fact, that her surgery isn't scheduled till next month."

"How's she doing?"

"Better than me," Neveah admitted ruefully. "Mama's always been very strong and stoic. Thankfully, she's not in any pain and has no symptoms. Did you know that she and your uncle are leaving tomorrow for Ireland?"

Xavier smiled. "Yeah, War told me. Good for them. I hope they have a great time together."

"Me, too. Mama could definitely use a relaxing getaway." Resettling her head on Xavier's shoulder, Neveah smiled softly. "I don't make a habit of discussing my mother's sex life, but I hope Randall gives her plenty of mind-blowing orgasms."

Xavier chuckled. "Nothing like some sexual healing."

"Absolutely."

He kissed her forehead, then stroked a hand down the curve of her back. "Let me know if there's anything you or your mama need."

"I will," Neveah promised.

A somber silence lapsed between them.

"Xay?"

"Yeah, baby?" he murmured.

"Can I ask you something?"

"Anything."

She hesitated, gnawing her lip. "If you'd met me and Jordan at the same time, would you still have chosen me?"

His hand stilled on her back. "Where did *that* question come from?"

Neveah shrugged. "I'm just curious."

"Really?" He sounded skeptical. "So after all these years, you're suddenly curious about whether I find your best friend attractive?"

Again she shrugged. "Maybe I've *always* been curious. Any woman who says she's never wondered the same thing is probably lying. And I noticed you haven't answered the question."

"That's because it's ridiculous," he said mildly. "But I'll humor you anyway. Hell, *yeah,* I still would have chosen you if I'd met you and Jordan at the same time. As far as I'm concerned, that's a no-brainer."

"Why?" Neveah countered. "Jordan's a beautiful woman."

"Sure," Xavier agreed. "And so are you. *More* beautiful, actually."

Neveah frowned. "I wasn't fishing for compliments."

"I know. But I'm just speaking the truth. Seriously, Neveah, your friend doesn't do anything for me."

"So you don't think you could ever be attracted to her?"

"Nope."

Neveah lifted her head and studied him, waiting for him to elaborate.

He did, albeit reluctantly. "I mean, you've seen me and Jordan hug once or twice over the years, right? When you guys graduated from college, or something like that. So that means we've had—" he paused, searching for the right word, trying to be tactful "—physical contact."

Neveah's lips twitched. "Meaning you've felt her breasts against your chest," she translated bluntly.

Xavier coughed into his hand. "Um…yeah. That's, uh, generally what happens during a hug. So, yeah, we've had physical contact before. And I felt absolutely nothing. So, no, I could never be attracted to her."

Now teasing him, Neveah prodded, "Just because you weren't turned on during a hug—"

Xavier gave her a pointed look. "The first day you and I met, when you gave me a hug for getting your mom's car started, I drove all the way home with a raging hard-on."

Neveah choked out a laugh. *"You did not!"*

"I did. For real." His eyes glimmered with amusement. "I had to hide from my family until it went away, or I never would have heard the end of it from Zeke."

Neveah's howl of laughter was joined by Xavier's.

Sobering after a few moments, he gazed at her intently, his hands cradling her face with infinite tenderness. "You never need to worry about how beautiful you are to me. I love everything about you, Neveah Symon. Everything from this—" he trailed a fingertip from the arch of her eyebrow "—to this." He ended with a gentle tap to her dimpled chin. "I love the way you talk, the way you walk, the way you smile, the way you laugh. I love the way you look when you're painting, and the way you blush when you're having an orgasm. I love that you're a mama's girl and damn proud of it. I love your feisty temper, the way your eyes shoot fire and you throw your hands on your hips whenever you're pissed off. I love how caring and sensitive you are, and how passionately you defend your beliefs." His voice softened. "If you haven't guessed by now, what I'm trying to say is that I love *you*."

Neveah stared at him, tears burning the backs of her eyes, her heart expanding until she thought it might burst from her rib cage. Their gazes clung for several long, electrifying moments.

"Neveah—"

Abruptly she rolled away from him and climbed out of the huge bed, murmuring, "I need to use the restroom."

She made her way quickly across the bedroom, grateful for the moonlit darkness that obscured her nudity. Once inside the luxurious master bathroom, she shut the door and sagged against it, cupping a hand over her mouth to stifle an anguished sob.

How can he do this to her? she wondered. *How can he look into her eyes and say the kind of things that unravel her soul?*

After several moments, Xavier spoke from the other side of the door. "Are you all right?" he asked gently.

Hastily scraping tears from the corners of her eyes, Neveah padded across the heated marble floor and called back, "I'm fine. I just have to pee."

His silence told her he didn't believe her.

So she sat on the toilet and willed her bladder to cooperate. "Really nice bathroom," she chatted conversationally, blinking rapidly to chase away the traitorous tears. "Travertine marble, spa shower, electronic faucets, plasma TV." She whistled appreciatively. "I could just camp out in here all night."

Which isn't such a bad idea, she thought grimly.

"Are you hungry?" Xavier asked quietly. "I was going to heat up the dinner my housekeeper left for me. She always makes more than enough."

"You have a housekeeper?"

"Yeah. She comes a few times a week, helps me out with some cooking and cleaning. So…yes to dinner?"

"Thanks, but I already ate with my mother." Neveah rose from the toilet and wiped herself, then flushed and crossed to the sink to wash her hands. "It's getting late. I should go."

"I'd rather you stayed."

Her belly quivered at the husky invitation in his voice. She braced her hands on the marble countertop and bowed her head, praying for the willpower to resist temptation, although she knew she'd long since passed the point of no return.

"At least keep me company while I eat," he cajoled.

She drew a deep, steadying breath. "Xay—"

"There's a clean robe in the linen cabinet if you want to put it on. I'd rather you didn't cover up, but…" He trailed off with a wicked chuckle. "Anyway, I'll be right back. I'm gonna get our things from the porch."

When he returned to the bedroom a few minutes later, she was wrapped in a plush blue robe that hung nearly to her feet. Perched on a mahogany bench at the foot of his bed, she tried not to stare at his magnificent chest as he sauntered across the room toward her. He'd pulled on a pair of long dark shorts that rode low on his hips. He was holding her purse, along with a bottle of champagne and two wineglasses.

She arched a brow at the latter items, but before she could comment, her cell phone rang. She dug it out of her purse and checked caller ID, smiling when she saw Yasmin's number.

Seeing her reaction, Xavier frowned, his eyes narrowing suspiciously. "Who's that?"

Your sister, Neveah mouthed, rolling her eyes at his possessive tone before she answered the phone. "Hey, Yasmin."

"Hi, Neveah." Yasmin's voice sounded hushed, as if she were trying not to be overheard. Most likely by her mother, who'd probably need an exorcist if she knew where Neveah was right now. "I hope I'm not disturbing you."

"Not at all."

"I couldn't wait until tomorrow to find out whether you saw Xay."

Neveah glanced up at the man in question, unnerved by how close he stood to her, so close that she could count the muscled ridges of his six-pack. She swallowed drily. "Um, yeah, I did see him."

"Oh, good!" Yasmin hesitated. "How's he doing?"

"He's…fine." *That was an understatement!*

Xavier touched her face, winking at her. "Tell her I'm *better* than fine."

Overhearing her brother's voice, Yasmin exclaimed in surprise, "Oh, you're still there?"

Heat stung Neveah's cheeks. "Y-yes, but I was just about to—"

Grinning mischievously, Xavier uncorked the bottle of champagne with a soft *whoosh.* Neveah stared at the foam spilling from the mouth and running down the side of the bottle. When her gaze dropped—inexplicably—to his crotch, she blushed furiously and jerked backward.

Xavier laughed, dark and downright wicked.

"Did someone just open a bottle of bubbly?" Yasmin asked excitedly.

Watching as Xavier poured champagne into the two glasses, Neveah sighed. "Your brother did."

Yasmin laughed, a warm, delighted sound. "Well, let me not keep you, then. It sounds like you two are having a *wonderful* time." Her voice softened. "Thank you, Neveah."

Her heart stirred at the quiet gratitude in the other woman's voice. "Don't mention it," she said gruffly.

After she'd hung up and put away her phone, Xavier handed her a glass of champagne and sat beside her on the bench, closer than she would have preferred.

"What's this for?" she asked warily, indicating her glass.

He smiled. "I was saving it for tomorrow night, but since you're already here, now's as good a time as any to celebrate."

"Celebrate what?"

Eyes twinkling, he crooned softly, *"Reunited and it feels so good—"*

"We're not reunited!"

He glanced meaningfully at the rumpled bed.

Her face flamed, and he laughed. "A toast," he proposed, raising his glass to her.

Holding his gaze, she reluctantly held up her own chilled flute. "To…?"

His expression gentled. "Second chances."

Neveah's heart thudded.

He stared at her, waiting for her to reciprocate.

After several prolonged moments, during which she debated the wisdom of accepting his toast—and all that it implied—she clinked her glass to his.

Something like relief, mingled with triumph, flashed in his eyes.

And she knew, like never before, that she was in trouble.

As they drank slowly, she stared at the facing wall, where he'd hung her *Golden Ecstasy* painting. She couldn't help noting that he'd mounted it perfectly, at eye level with small accent lights that helped the painting "pop" off the wall without leaving any shadows.

Following the direction of her gaze, Xavier murmured, "What're you thinking about?"

"How well you mounted the painting. Not many people know the proper way to do it."

"I learned from the best. Or don't you remember teaching me years ago?"

Neveah met his gaze, surprised and undeniably pleased. "I didn't think you were paying attention."

"Of course I was."

They smiled at each other.

Returning her gaze to the painting, Neveah grinned wryly. "Jordan told me the buyer was going to hang the piece in her bedroom. Is that what you told her?"

"No," Xavier drawled, mouth twitching, "but what better place for a painting like that?"

"Meaning?"

"Meaning it's sexy as hell, Neveah."

"Hmm." She regarded the nude couple she'd captured on canvas, their glistening brown limbs entwined in a way that made it impossible to tell where one ended and the other began.

Xavier was also studying the painting, his head cocked at a thoughtful angle. "I've been wondering…" he murmured.

Neveah didn't want to ask, but she had to. "Wondering what?"

A slight smile played at the edges of his lips. "I've been wondering what you were thinking about when you painted that." He turned his head, meeting her gaze. "Or rather, *who* you were thinking about."

Neveah glanced away, forcing a nonchalant shrug. "I wasn't thinking about anyone. It's just a painting."

"Bull," he countered softly. "It's *never* just a painting for you."

She said nothing, because she knew he was right.

"As soon as I saw it," he continued, setting down his wineglass, "I couldn't help but notice the couple's resemblance to us."

"Oh, please, that's ridiculous," Neveah scoffed. "You can't see that. They're mostly in silhouette."

"Their complexions are the same as ours," Xavier pointed out. "And the man's hair is cornrowed, just like mine used to be—"

"Plenty of Senegalese men wear their hair braided," she interjected.

"—and he has a goatee. While the woman's hair is also braided—"

"Unlike mine."

"—she has a tiny mole *right* there." He reached out, trailing a finger from Neveah's throat down to the valley between her full breasts. As she shivered from his gossamer touch, his lips curved in a slow, satisfied smile. "Just like you."

She gulped. "Coincidence."

His eyes glinted. "I don't think so."

Snatching the lapels of her robe together, she snapped, "How did you notice such a small detail anyway?"

He grinned. "I've been studying that painting for the past three days. I can see it when I close my eyes at night. It's definitely stirred my…imagination."

"Congratulations," Neveah grumbled. "You got your money's worth."

"Absolutely." He chuckled. "So I have to ask. Did you?"

She tensed. "Did I what?"

"Imagine us. When you created *Golden Ecstasy,* did you imagine us?"

Neveah shivered at the deep, velvety timbre of his voice. Her face flushed, and her blood suddenly felt as hot as the scorching sun she'd depicted in the painting.

It was one thing to have poured out her innermost longings and desires in the privacy of her own home. She'd even been amused to hear the piece discussed and dissected by perfect strangers. But, now, to sit here beside the very man who'd inspired such lustful cravings and fantasies… It was simply too much.

"I think you did imagine us," Xavier whispered seductively. "Which means you've been dreaming about me, wanting me, *aching* for me, as much as I have you."

Oh God, Neveah thought as her nipples tightened and molten heat pooled between her thighs.

She didn't resist as he leaned down and slanted his lips over hers in a deep, drugging kiss that sent violent pulses of sensation rushing to her loins. As his tongue delved inside her mouth, sensually tangling with hers, a low moan shuddered past her lips.

Her head went back as he pulled her slowly onto his lap, his lips stroking the throbbing pulse points along her exposed throat. Even through the thick layer of the robe, she could feel the hard, scorching length of his erection against her butt.

Without opening her eyes, she whispered shakily, "You're gonna make me spill my champagne."

"Then put down the glass," came his husky command.

She shook her head, foolishly thinking that her refusal would stop this dangerous interlude before it went any further.

When he reached around her, she moved the glass out of reach, sloshing champagne on the floor.

He chuckled softly, the sound sending tremors through her body. "So that's how you wanna do this. All right."

As he dipped his tongue into her ear, she shivered with arousal. Slowly his hands moved up her rib cage, cupping and kneading her breasts. She groaned as, once again, the robe proved to be no barrier between them. As her breathing quickened, he untied the belt and dragged it off her shoulders, exposing her breasts to the cool air. Her nipples puckered as his big, calloused hands covered them, teasing and stroking the turgid peaks until she moaned and writhed against him.

He kissed his way down her bare shoulders, making her shudder as he scraped his teeth against her sensitized flesh. A full, throbbing ache flooded her loins.

Suddenly he lifted her from his lap with an economy of motion and turned her around to straddle his thighs. The fabric of his shorts rasped the plump folds of her sex as she ground herself against his bulging erection. More drops of wine spilled.

"We're making…a mess," she panted.

He sucked her lower lip. "*Your* fault. I told you to put down the damn glass."

"A-all right," she stammered breathlessly. "Y-you can… take it."

"I thought so." He snagged the glass from her trembling hand and took a lazy sip before bathing her naked breasts with the remaining champagne. She gasped sharply as he sent the empty glass hurtling across the room and crashing into the fireplace.

"Nice shot," she breathed. "But I see you like breaking things."

He flashed a crooked half grin before bending his head to lick her dripping breasts. The lash of his hot tongue, contrasted with the chilled wine, made her cry out in shocked pleasure. He pushed her nipples together and drew them into his mouth, gently biting and sucking them until her whole body shook uncontrollably.

Abruptly he lifted her off his lap, stripped the robe from her body and turned her around. "Bend over so I can taste you," he whispered roughly.

She obeyed at once. With her butt planted in the air, her hands braced on the floor and her legs splayed apart, she felt like they were playing some erotic version of Twister.

"Damn," Xavier purred. "You always did have the most bodacious booty."

"Don't play with me," Neveah warned, husky with arousal.

"I wouldn't dare." He slid off the bench and crouched behind her. She jerked in surprise as his tongue licked the underside of her butt before sliding higher, drawing out her torture and heightening her anticipation. By the time she felt his breath against her labia, her thighs were quaking so hard it was almost embarrassing.

When he flicked his tongue against the hood of her clitoris, she let out a smothered cry. As blood rushed straight from her head to her engorged clit, he pressed his open mouth to her sex and suckled her.

"Xay...Xay..." she stuttered insensibly.

He feasted on her, alternately licking her labia and nibbling her clit until she came in undulating waves, shuddering and mewling. He moved back onto the bench and yanked down his shorts, then lifted her effortlessly and stood her astride his lap, with her back to him. He groaned thickly as she sheathed him with the condom he'd already removed from his pants pocket.

As he lowered her onto his jutting erection, she spread her thighs wide, sinking deeper until he was fully embedded. His hands gripped her waist, anchoring her in place as he began a slow, sensual glide. She moaned and closed her eyes, wondering how she'd survived so many years without experiencing the sheer ecstasy of his lovemaking.

As he increased the tempo of his strokes, she arched her back, provocatively thrusting her ass onto his shaft. He slapped her butt, and she cried out.

"So you didn't imagine us when you created that painting," he challenged, low and guttural.

"I...d-didn't—"

"Liar." The soft rebuke was punctuated by another slap that made her quiver.

As that same hand reached up to massage her aching breast, she turned her head, seeking his mouth. They shared a long, carnal kiss that left them both groaning.

He began thrusting harder and deeper, hitting her in spots no man had ever come close to approaching. She rocked her hips, breasts bouncing as he bucked under her, taking her with a ferocity that had her gasping. She reached behind her, grabbing the back of his neck and holding on tight as his hips pummeled her backside with sharp slaps that echoed around the room.

His lips skated up the curve of her neck to her ear. "Look at that painting," he commanded, pointing to the wall.

She obeyed, though her eyes were so glazed the image was a blur.

He reached between her thighs, cupping her where their bodies were joined. "I want you to look at that painting and imagine us, like this, for the rest of our lives."

She erupted with a loud, keening wail, convulsed in the grip of the most breathtakingly violent orgasm she'd ever had. As her body's rapid, pulsing spasms clutched at Xavier's penis, he grabbed her hips and thrust one last time, forceful enough to lift her off his lap. And then he came with a hoarse, exultant shout.

They remained locked together for several moments, bodies trembling, mouths parted as they panted harshly.

As their breathing gradually returned to normal, Xavier turned his head and kissed her, soft, sweet and slow. When he would have moved away, her lips clung to his, not wanting to let go.

"Spend the night," he whispered.

This time, she didn't even *think* about refusing.

Chapter 16

The next morning, Xavier strolled through the entrance of the community center's cafeteria. The large hall, which had been modeled after a solarium, was enclosed with glass walls and decorated with lush plants and palm trees. It was a favorite gathering place of the staff and children, who received free breakfast and lunch under the center's nutrition program. Now that school was back in session, the facility was mostly populated by day-care children and the senior citizens who took advantage of the center's adult learning courses. The older kids showed up in droves after school.

As Xavier strode across the cafeteria, the bright sunshine beaming through the windows could have been powered by his buoyant mood. After the incredible night of passion he and Neveah had shared, he was on top of the world. Not only had they connected physically—*and, man, had they ever!*—he also sensed that he'd broken through some of her emotional barriers, as well. Although he knew he still had his work cut out for him, he felt hopeful that he was on the right track to reclaiming her love. Adding to his euphoria that morning was the fact that he wouldn't have to wait long to see her again. Neveah was due to arrive any minute for the tour he'd promised her, which had him more excited than a rich kid counting down the days until Christmas.

After emerging from the cafeteria line with two covered cups of coffee, Xavier was headed back to his office to wait for Neveah when a chorus of childish voices rang out, "Good morning, Professor X!"

When he glanced around and saw a table full of preschoolers waving animatedly at him, his face broke into a wide grin. As he turned and started toward the table, one small girl darted out of her chair and raced toward him, defying her teacher's command to remain seated.

Xavier laughed as the child launched herself at him, throwing her arms around his legs.

"Janessa!" admonished her exasperated teacher. "I told you not to—"

"That's okay, Kristen. Here, hold these for me." After handing over the two coffee cups, Xavier reached down and scooped up the little girl, making her squeal with delight as he hoisted her into the air before hugging her.

"Hey, baby girl," he greeted her warmly. "Enjoying your breakfast?"

She bobbed her head, making her colorful barrettes bounce. "I'm eating *pancakes.*"

"Mmmm. I love pancakes."

"But not with syrup." She screwed up her face. "I hate syrup. *Yuck!*"

Xavier laughed, affectionately tweaking her nose. While every child who came to the community center was important to him, he couldn't deny that Janessa held a special place in his heart. With her angelic face, mocha coloring and dimpled chin, she could have been Neveah's daughter. The first time he ever saw her, he'd been dumbstruck by the uncanny resemblance. Learning that her parents had been tragically killed during a burglary had made the little girl even more endearing to him. If there hadn't been a doting aunt in the picture, Xavier would have seriously considered adopting Janessa and recruiting his sisters to help him raise her.

As Janessa fiddled with his tie, Kristen apologized to Xavier, "I'm so sorry they called you Professor X. I've told them to address you as Mr. Mayne, but you know how much they like to imitate the older kids."

Xavier chuckled. "It's all good," he assured her, reaching down to palm the melon-sized head of another little boy, who beamed at him. "I don't mind the nickname. It's actually a compliment."

Kristen gave him a shy smile.

"Oh, darling! Yoo-hoo!"

Glancing up, Xavier saw his mother, Zeke and Yolanda having breakfast at a table near the back. As Birdie waved him over, Zeke made a slashing motion across his throat, warning Xavier to keep his distance.

Suppressing a grimace, Xavier kissed the top of Janessa's head and gently lowered her into her chair. "Be good," he told her with a wink.

"Okay." She winked back.

Grinning, Xavier retrieved his drinks from Kristen and started toward his family.

When he reached them, Zeke and Yolanda rose from the table muttering excuses about needing to return to work. Before departing, Yolanda patted Xavier's cheek and smiled at him, while Zeke clapped him on the shoulder and leaned close to advise, "Don't say nothing, bruh. Just nod your head and pretend to listen."

Xavier chuckled as his siblings beat a hasty retreat, shooting him sympathetic glances over their shoulders.

"Hey, baby," Birdie said warmly. She was dressed in designer workout clothes for her Pilates class, which she took four times a week at the community center.

"Hey, Ma." Xavier bent to kiss her upturned cheek before joining her at the table.

She arched an amused brow at the two cups of coffee he'd set down. "Long day ahead?"

Xavier could have laughed at the joke and left it at that, but he'd already decided to level with his mother about his intentions toward Neveah. The sooner he set her straight, the better off everyone would be.

"Actually," he replied, "one of these is for Neveah. I'm expecting her any minute, so I can't stay long."

"I see." Birdie's lips thinned with displeasure. "Well, while we're on the subject, I've been meaning to talk to you about her."

Nodding slowly, Xavier murmured, "Speak your mind, Ma, and then I'm gonna speak mine."

"All right. I think it would be a mistake for you to allow that girl—"

"Woman."

"—back into your life after the way she hurt you. If she couldn't see how special you were all those years ago, then she doesn't deserve a second chance with you. I never really trusted her to begin with, but I held my tongue because I knew how much she meant to you. But don't ask me to stand by and watch her break your heart again, because I won't do it. I can't."

When she'd finished speaking, Xavier asked calmly, "Are you finished?"

Birdie's chin lifted in defiance. "For the moment."

"All right, then. My turn." He reached across the table and gently took her hand. "I love you, Ma. I know the pain you went through with my father, and I appreciate everything you've ever done for me and my siblings. You're a proud, strong woman who'd fight to the death to protect her children. But the truth is, you're wrong about Neveah. She saw something in me from the very beginning. Something that enabled her to put up with my baggage a lot longer than most people would have. Yeah, she hurt me when she broke up with me and left without saying goodbye. But you know what, Ma? I hurt her, too. I can't undo the past, but now that Neveah's back in my life, I don't intend to lose her again. I love her, Ma, and nothing's gonna stop me from being with her if she'll have me."

By the time he'd finished his heartfelt declaration, tears were glistening in his mother's eyes. "This isn't easy for me," she whispered.

"I know."

"I almost lost you that day. You could have died—"

"But I didn't," Xavier interrupted gently. "You took care of me, and I lived. Lived to drive you crazy with my troublemaking antics. Lived to meet the woman of my dreams."

When Birdie rolled her eyes in exasperation, he smiled. "The more you reject her, the more you're gonna have to backtrack when she and I get married."

"Married?" Birdie sputtered. "She hasn't even been back that long, and you're already talking about *marrying* her?"

His lips twitched. "I'm working on it."

"Lord have mercy," Birdie muttered under her breath. "I still think you're taking a big risk."

"It's worth taking." Xavier paused. "If Warrick had listened to all of us, he and Raina wouldn't be together now. And I think we both know that would have been an absolute travesty."

Birdie's mouth tightened, the flash of guilt in her eyes speaking volumes.

Xavier squeezed her hand, then rose from the table and picked up his drinks. "I should go. I don't want to keep Neveah waiting."

Birdie sighed. "You can have any woman you want, Xay. Why do you have to have *that* one?"

"Because she's the only one I've ever wanted," he said simply.

With that, he turned and headed out of the cafeteria.

As he neared the doorway, he saw Neveah standing there, waiting for him. His heart leaped into his throat at the sight of her. She looked incredibly beautiful and earthy in a kente-patterned tank top and dark jeans that molded her long, curvy legs. At the memory of those luscious legs wrapped around him as he thrust into her, his groin heated. Catching the wicked glint in his eyes, Neveah blushed.

"Hey," she said demurely.

"Hey, yourself."

"Your assistant told me where to find you." She swept a glance around the cafeteria. If she saw his mother, she gave no indication. "What a gorgeous dining hall."

"Thanks. We enjoy it." He passed her one of the coffee cups. "Hope it's still warm."

She sipped from the opening in the lid. "It's perfect. Thank you."

"You're welcome." He offered his arm. "Ready for your tour?"

She smiled, tucking her hand through his arm. "What I've seen so far—" She broke off abruptly, staring over his shoulder at something that had caught her eye.

Turning his head, Xavier saw that Kristen was leading her flock of preschoolers out of the cafeteria. Keeping her promise to behave, Janessa was dutifully marching along in single file. But as she neared the doorway, she glanced over at Xavier and Neveah. With an impish gleam in her eyes, she lifted her hand and waved.

As they waved back, Neveah whispered, "Who is that little girl?"

"Her name's Janessa." Xavier smiled, slanting Neveah a sidelong glance. "Does she remind you of anyone?"

She swallowed and shook her head, but he sensed that she was lying.

Over the next two hours, he gave her a complete tour of the sprawling community center. Not counting the outdoor amenities, the facility included two indoor gymnasiums, a fitness center, a dance studio, a racquetball court and an Olympic-size pool. He pointed out the newly added day-care center, and explained the broad range of recreational and educational activities that were offered to the community. Neveah was clearly impressed as she asked questions and lingered to admire everything. At one point they stopped to chat with the Blackwells, who were on their way to swimming class. As Xavier admired Neveah's natural ease with the elderly couple, he prayed that he would be lucky enough to grow old with her. When he showed her the large hall he'd chosen for the mural's location, he watched as she took careful measure of the area, assessing the skylight ceiling and other dimensions in a manner that filled him with hope.

"The center is absolutely amazing," she marveled as they headed up to the third floor at the end of the tour. Xavier was taking her to his office, where he already had a contract prepared should she decide to do the mural. "You and your brothers thought of everything, and then some."

Xavier smiled. "We definitely tried to."

"You did. And I think it's wonderful that you and your siblings are able to work together."

"You mean without killing one another?" he teased.

Neveah laughed.

As they reached his office, Xavier unlocked the door and gestured her inside. "Welcome to my home away from—"

Neveah gasped sharply, staring across the large room with an arrested expression.

Following the direction of her gaze, Xavier saw what had captured her attention. Prominently displayed on the wall behind his desk was one of her most popular works of art, a portrait of a hauntingly beautiful little girl running through a lush field of lavender.

"Lavender Nymph," Neveah breathed.

Xavier nodded, smiling poignantly as he gazed upon the painting. "It's my favorite portrait of yours."

"How did you...when did you..." She trailed off, too stunned to finish.

But Xavier understood. "You're wondering how I got the original."

"Yes," she whispered.

He smiled. "Well, as you probably know, the original buyer was the widow of a wealthy philanthropist. When she passed away a few years ago, her funeral was covered by all the local media. It was reported that her children intended to donate her art collection to a museum. When I learned that she owned *Lavender Nymph,* I went to the family and told them I wanted to buy the painting from them, and I was willing to pay whatever they wanted. But they weren't interested in money. They said they were honoring their mother's wishes by donating her cherished art collection." His voice softened. "I was desperate, so I decided to lay all my cards on the table. I told them that I was in love with the artist, and whenever I looked at her painting—"

"No," Neveah whimpered so softly he barely heard her.

"—I imagined that the lavender nymph was the child I wish we'd had together."

Swallowing tightly, he hazarded a look at Neveah. When

he saw tears shimmering in her eyes, he instantly knew he'd revealed too much, too soon.

"Neveah?" he said gently. "Baby, are you—"

She shook her head as she backed toward the door, looking as though she'd seen a ghost. "I—I have to go."

"Now? But I was hoping we could—"

"I can't. I can't."

Torn between confusion and guilt, Xavier watched as she turned and fled from the room.

It took everything he had not to follow her.

Several hours later, Neveah lay curled on her side in the darkness of her bedroom. After fleeing the community center that morning, she'd made it as far as the next block before she broke down, racked by sobs that forced her to pull over before she caused an accident. She barely even remembered driving home.

Her emotions had been on shaky ground ever since she saw the little girl named Janessa. She'd been stunned by the child's uncanny resemblance to the sweet-faced cherub depicted in her painting, but somehow she'd managed to maintain her composure and enjoy the tour of the community center. She couldn't have known what awaited her in Xavier's office, a surprise discovery that would plunge her back into a bottomless abyss of heartache and grief.

Closing her eyes, Neveah opened herself to the memories of the day she'd created *Lavender Nymph*. She'd traveled to Provence, France and had been staying at a quaint manor house nestled in a countryside village. The day after her arrival, armed with her paint and easel, she'd ventured out to a field bursting with wild lavender. She'd only intended to capture the scenic landscape, but as she began sketching, she'd found herself envisioning a small child in a white dress, laughing and dashing through the lush, purple forest.

It was the child she'd always dreamed of having with Xavier. The child she'd lost, but had never forgotten.

She began sketching furiously, heedless of the tears streaming down her face or the sun that gradually sank behind the hills. By the time she'd finished painting, she was physically and emotionally drained. But the experience had been cathartic, giving her one of the first moments of joy she'd felt in three years. She'd kept the painting until an elderly Senegalese neighbor told her about the healing power of releasing the spirits of departed loved ones. After that, Neveah reluctantly sold *Lavender Nymph,* never imagining that the portrait would catapult her to international stardom and become her most celebrated work of art.

It seemed inconceivable, and tragically ironic, that Xavier was now in possession of the painting. What were the odds that fate would conspire against her in such a manner? She'd never intended to tell him about her miscarriage, but now she would be forever haunted by the words he'd spoken to her earlier. *Whenever I looked at her painting, I imagined that the lavender nymph was the child I wish we'd had together.*

Neveah exhaled a deep, shuddering breath and curled into a tighter ball. Her cell phone rang from her purse, but she ignored it, as she'd been doing all day. She knew Xavier had been calling her, undoubtedly wondering why she'd fled from his office as though the devil were on her heels.

For the first time ever, she seriously considered the possibility that she'd been wrong to keep him in the dark all these years. After the car accident, she'd been devastated and humiliated by his betrayal, and the *last* thing she'd wanted him to know was how close she'd come to giving up her artistic ambitions to have his baby. But the burden of keeping such a painful secret had been slowly ravaging her.

Suddenly Raina's words drifted through her mind. *I know what it's like to be confronted with a past you've been trying to forget. And I also know how impossible it is to keep running.*

Neveah had been running for thirteen years, but she'd gotten nowhere. Maybe it was time for her to release the spirits of the past that had been tormenting her. Maybe it was time for her to forgive, and allow her fractured soul to be healed.

And then maybe, just maybe, she could be whole again.

Chapter 17

After suffering through a long, sleepless night and then an endless series of morning meetings, Xavier received the most unexpected gift when he arrived at the community center the next afternoon.

Neveah was there, quietly at work on the mural.

He couldn't see her at first. According to his siblings— who'd met him at the front entrance when he arrived—Neveah had showed up that morning with her art supplies and an army of assistants who'd erected a large scaffold that ran the length of the wall. The curtained platform concealed Neveah, as well as her work, from view.

As Xavier entered the hall, he called out tentatively, "Neveah?"

"Don't come back here," she warned, her voice muffled. "I don't want anyone to see the mural until it's finished."

"Not even me?"

"*Especially* not you."

For the first time since yesterday, Xavier smiled. "Can you at least come out so I can see you?"

"Not right now. I'm busy."

His smile widened. How well he remembered that distracted, slightly irritated tone of hers whenever she was absorbed in her work.

"We need to discuss your commission," he said. "I have a contract—"

"I don't want payment."

He frowned. "Neveah, you're a famous artist—"

"Which means I don't need the money," she said pragmatically. Before he could protest further, she added, "Consider this my modest contribution to your worthy cause. My gift to the community."

Xavier closed his eyes, his heart swelling with such love and gratitude he thought he'd drown in it. "There's nothing remotely 'modest' about your contribution," he told her, his voice husky with emotion.

Neveah said nothing.

Although he knew better than to look a gift horse in the mouth, he couldn't resist asking, "What changed your mind?"

More silence.

And then he heard a shuffling sound, as if she were climbing a set of steps. A moment later, her beautiful face appeared above the platform, her eyes bright with unshed tears.

When their gazes met, she whispered, "It was the lavender nymph."

Over the next two weeks, they became as inseparable as they'd ever been. Although Xavier had promised not to disturb Neveah while she worked, he couldn't seem to stay away—and she didn't want him to. She looked forward to his daily visits, during which he brought her lunch, then lingered to keep her company while she ate. They talked about everything. She captivated him with stories about the Senegalese people and culture, and he brought her up to speed on everything that had happened to his family over the years. She was saddened to hear about Yolanda's incarceration, but was glad to see that she'd gotten her life back on track and made amends with Raina.

She received yet another shock when Xavier revealed to her that Randall was Warrick's father, courtesy of a brief affair he'd once had with Birdie.

"My mom mentioned something about your mother giving her and Randall evil looks at the picnic. No wonder." Neveah grimaced. "As if Birdie needed *another* reason to hate me."

Xavier chuckled. "Don't worry, sweetheart. Ma's not gonna give you any more trouble."

Neveah wasn't entirely convinced of that, but she appreciated the reassurance anyway.

Once, when she'd been painting late into the evening, Xavier surprised her by rolling in a linen-covered table aglow with soft candlelight. They dined on filet mignon while listening to old Babyface songs, a tender tribute to the first night they'd ever made love. When Xavier took her into his arms for a dreamy slow dance, she felt as beautiful and alluring as if she were wearing Versace and diamonds instead of paint-spattered denim. And just as they'd done that night years ago, they consummated their romantic dinner with passionate lovemaking—this time in the small heated pool located inside the aquatics center.

At his insistence, she spent every night at his house so they could commute together to the community center. After dinner every night, they cuddled on the porch swing and watched the sun set over the lake. With each passing day, Neveah felt herself growing more attached to the beautiful ranch, as well as its owner.

One evening when they arrived home, Xavier blindfolded her and led her around to the back. She thought he was taking her to the guest cottage, since it was the only place they hadn't christened. But when he removed her blindfold, they were standing inside one of the small outbuildings that the previous owner had used as a storage shed. To Neveah's shocked delight, the space had been converted into an art studio, complete with walls of windows that allowed ample lighting, a worktable for sketching and shelves for storing paint supplies and equipment. There was even a wood-burning fireplace to keep her warm during the winter.

Stunned, she gaped at Xavier. "How on earth did you pull this off when I've been here every day?"

He smiled. "The contractors came during the day while we weren't here. Do you like it?"

"Like it? I *love* it. It's…it's perfect!" Bursting with gratitude, she leaped into his arms.

Laughing, he caught her around the waist, lifted her off the floor and twirled her around as she clung to his neck.

Meeting his eyes, she whispered, "Thank you."

His gaze gentled. "I'd do anything for you, Neveah. *Anything.*"

At the end of their second week together, Neveah's most recent artwork was introduced with great fanfare at a charity auction to benefit cancer research. Her surprise appearance was met with thunderous applause by the attendees, which included a who's who of luminaries in the art world. As honored as she was to receive a standing ovation, it was the sight of Xavier in the audience, his eyes glowing with pride and adulation, that nearly brought her to her knees.

At the end of the evening, he outbid several other art collectors vying for ownership of her idyllic portrait of a Senegalese fisherman perched on a rock beside a giant pelican. Afterward, when Xavier strode to the stage to pose for photographs with Neveah, she leaned up to whisper in his ear, "Take me home."

Surprised, he met her gaze and whispered back, "Are you sure? Don't you need to stay and schmooze?"

"The only schmoozing I wanna do is with you, if you catch my drift." She wiggled her brows suggestively. "Now are you gonna take me home or what?"

A wolfish gleam filled his eyes. "With pleasure."

With camera bulbs flashing, and a wave of shocked gasps and laughter rippling through the audience, he swept her into his arms and carried her right out of the ballroom.

Not surprisingly, their dramatic exit was the subject of every local society column the next day, each article excitedly speculating on the steamy romance between Houston's most eligible bachelor and most famous artist.

After reciting an excerpt from the *Houston Chronicle,* Neveah set aside her BlackBerry with a sigh. "You've made me the gossip magnet of the art world."

Snuggled against her in bed, Xavier chuckled, nibbling her earlobe. "Guess you should have thought of that before you propositioned me in front of all those people."

"True." She grinned impishly. "Seth, my manager, couldn't be more thrilled with all the publicity. Jordan, on the other hand, says the phone's been ringing nonstop at the gallery. She doesn't sound very happy."

"Too bad."

"Meanie!"

They both laughed.

Sobering after a few moments, Neveah cradled Xavier's face between her hands and looked into his eyes. "Thank you for coming to the auction."

His expression softened. "Nothing could have kept me

away." He glanced down, his thick lashes shielding his eyes. "I want you to know that even though I stopped attending your college art shows, I never stopped caring…never stopped being proud of you."

Overcome with emotion, Neveah crushed her mouth to his. As the kiss exploded, no more words were spoken.

She pushed him onto his back, then knelt and took his shaft deep into her mouth. He groaned, shoving his fingers into her hair as she pleasured him, licking and sucking until he pulled out and rolled her over. He captured her wrists, pinning her hands above her head as his strong thighs parted hers.

Her lips opened on a soundless cry as he entered her, stretching her. They stared at each other as he began rocking inside her, spreading fire from her breasts to her aching sex. He lowered his mouth to hers but didn't kiss her, letting their breath mingle in a way that was powerfully erotic.

You belong to me, his gaze told her.

Always, her heart agreed.

In her mind's eye, she imagined how they looked together, their limbs sensuously entwined, the muscles in his back and buttocks contracting as he thrust into her. She wanted to paint them, wanted to immortalize this moment on canvas.

Because even as their bodies shattered in ecstasy, she feared that the bond they'd rediscovered wouldn't last forever.

Chapter 18

Two nights later, Xavier was awakened by a creaking noise.

He bolted upright, straining to listen.

After a few seconds, he heard the sound again.

He tossed aside the covers and rolled out of bed, striding purposefully to the oversize closet. Moments later he emerged with a loaded shotgun he'd removed from the gun vault. He'd purchased the weapon at the advice of the ranch's previous owner, who'd cautioned him to be prepared in case a mountain lion wandered onto the property.

As Xavier crept from the bedroom, he took comfort in the fact that Neveah was in New York, where she'd flown to headline another art auction. He'd never forgive himself if anything happened to her while she was here.

He moved silently through the dark house, nerves stretched taut. He could hear the wind rustling through the trees, and as he neared the front door, the creaking noise grew louder. But it no longer sounded like a wild animal prowling around in the darkness.

No, Xavier realized, his head tilted at an angle as he listened. The noise was coming from the porch.

Someone was rocking on the swing.

Pulse thudding, he quietly unlocked the front door, then cocked the shotgun and hefted it to his shoulder. A split second later he flipped on the light and burst onto the porch, his weapon aimed at the intruder.

Nothing could have prepared him for what he encountered.

Rocking back and forth on the swing, as though he had every right to be there, was a man Xavier hadn't seen in thirty years. A man he'd hoped never to see again.

Tariq Mayne.

Xavier's heart jackknifed into his throat and he staggered back a step, staring in shock. He was convinced that his eyes were deceiving him. But when he blinked, the tall, gaunt figure didn't disappear.

"What are you doing here?" Xavier whispered hoarsely.

His father chuckled. "Is that any way to greet your old man?"

"No." Raising the shotgun to eye level, Xavier took deadly aim. "This is."

Tariq went still, eyeing him nervously. "Come on, son. Put that thing down. You don't wanna shoot me."

"Wanna bet?" Xavier stared down the sights of his shotgun. "See this? It's a Mossberg 590, twelve gauge, fully loaded. One shot, and you'd be good and dead before your body hit the floor. You're trespassing on my property. Give me one damn reason I shouldn't pull this trigger."

Tariq held up trembling hands. "I'm not armed, Xay. You got no reason to shoot me."

"Bullshit," Xavier snarled. "I have *every* reason to shoot you. Why should I spare your sorry life when you never gave a damn about mine?"

"Th-That's not true," Tariq stammered. "I always felt that you and me had a special connection—"

Xavier's harsh bark of laughter cut him off. "The only thing you were connected to was your crack pipe. Or have you forgotten that you spent more time strung out on crack than actually being a husband and a father? Your warped idea of bonding was getting high with your six-year-old son. Remember that?"

Tariq faltered, nervously moistening his lips. "I had a problem—"

"And your *problem* nearly got me killed. If Ma hadn't gotten me to the hospital in time, I would have overdosed. I already had pneumonia. The doctor said the amount of cocaine I inhaled was enough to finish me off. Ma had to get down on her knees and beg the nurse not to call Child Protective Services, or they would have taken me away. Is that what you wanted? Or maybe you wanted me to become a junkie like you."

"I never meant for that to happen," Tariq insisted. "You have to believe—"

As he started to rise, Xavier growled, "Don't move, or so help me, God, I will blow your heart out and feed it to the vultures."

Gulping audibly, Tariq resettled on the swing. He hadn't aged well. His face was rawboned, with deep lines carved around his eyes and mouth, a shell of the handsome man he'd once been.

"Now, son—"

"Don't call me that," Xavier ground out. "I'm not your son. Your brother's been more of a father to me than you *ever* were."

Tariq sneered. "Good ol' Randall. He always liked to play the hero. But that self-righteous bastard had no qualms about laying with my wife and getting her pregnant. Cheating—"

"Don't talk about my mother!" Xavier roared. "She was a good wife to you. Better than you ever deserved. After all the women you ran through, you've got some damn nerve calling Ma a cheater. Say one more word about her, and it'll be your last."

Eyeing him fearfully, Tariq wisely shut up.

"What do you want?" Xavier demanded. "Why are you here?"

"I got nowhere else to go," Tariq mumbled.

"What do you mean?"

"I need a place to stay."

"Here's a suggestion," Xavier jeered. "Why don't you go back to that rock you crawled out from under?"

Tariq grimaced. "I know I deserved that—"

"And a whole lot worse." Xavier's shoulder had started to burn from the weight of the shotgun, but he didn't lower it, refusing to let down his guard physically or emotionally.

Tariq met his gaze. "You have every reason to hate me for walking out on you and your siblings. But I didn't have a choice. Your mama wanted me gone, and I owed people money. I was afraid they'd come after y'all if I didn't pay up, so I left and went to Dallas. I got clean, Xay. I even met a nice woman and started a new family."

Xavier didn't want to hear this, didn't want to feel an ounce of empathy for this man who'd robbed him of his innocence and nearly ruined his life. "So what happened?" he taunted. "How long did it take you to mess up *their* lives, too?"

Tariq's eyes shifted guiltily away. "Let's just say I traded one addiction for another. I started gambling, and when I lost all our money, she put me out. Even got a restraining order against me so I couldn't see the kids," he added bitterly. "I've been trying to land back on my feet ever since, but it's hard."

"So you came here looking for a handout," Xavier said flatly.

Tariq hesitated. "I've seen how well you and your brothers are doing. Warrick's got his family set up nicely in River Oaks. And you've got all this land out here, plus millions in the bank, from what I've heard. I figured you could give me a helping hand."

"You figured wrong," Xavier said coldly. "I want you gone by morning, or I'll have you arrested for trespassing."

"But I got nowhere else to go," Tariq said plaintively.

"That's not my problem."

Xavier marched into the house, slammed the door and returned to bed. But, of course, sleep eluded him.

Sometime in the middle of the night, he got up and retrieved a spare blanket, then stalked outside to the porch. His father was fast asleep, sprawled across the swing.

Xavier leaned down and covered him with the blanket. As he turned and walked back to the front door, Tariq called out humbly, "Thank you…son."

Xavier hesitated for several moments, then returned to the house without a backward glance.

Chapter 19

Something was wrong.

It had been three days since Neveah returned from New York, and she'd hardly seen or spoken to Xavier. He was distant. Preoccupied. When he wasn't away at meetings, he mostly confined himself to his office. It was Yasmin and Yolanda who came to the hall where she was painting and tag-teamed her into taking lunch breaks with them. And it was Xavier—not Neveah—who suggested that she resume sleeping at her own house so that she could accompany her mother to her pre-op appointments.

Once, when Neveah cornered him and asked him what was going on, he'd told her that he was just busy with work. But she didn't believe him. Something had changed with him, although she didn't know what. She was afraid to find out that another woman had come between them—again.

On the third day, she headed upstairs to his office to ask him a question about the mural, which was nearly complete. When she arrived, his assistant informed her that Xavier was conducting a job interview. Moments later, the door opened and Alyson Kelley emerged wearing a cleavage-baring blouse and an inappropriately short skirt. Smoothing her hair, she shot Neveah a smug glance before strutting away.

Eyes narrowed suspiciously, Neveah looked inside Xavier's office. He was on the phone, absently straightening his tie. Glimpsing her in the doorway, he held up one finger, signaling that he'd be with her in a minute.

She left without a word.

Two hours later, she was at her art gallery reviewing one of Topaz's latest abstracts to be put on sale. She was complimenting him on his staining technique when, without warning, he leaned over and kissed her.

"Whoa!" she exclaimed, jerking away from him. "What was *that* for?"

He smiled. "I just wanted to show my appreciation for all you've done for me, taking time to provide feedback on my work and giving me all this valuable exposure."

"A simple 'thank you' would have sufficed," Neveah muttered.

"Not really." He chuckled. "I've been wanting to do that for a while. You already know that I'm a huge admirer of yours, Neveah. I'm also very attracted to you."

"*Excuse* me?" she sputtered, staring at him as though he'd lost his mind. "You're supposed to be dating Jordan, who also happens to be my best friend."

He made a sour face. "Yeah, well, it didn't work out. And you might want to rethink your definition of 'best friend.'"

Neveah frowned. "What are you talking—"

"What's going on here?"

They glanced up to find Jordan standing in the doorway of the storage space that had been converted into Neveah's office. Her eyes were narrowed as she divided a speculative glance between Neveah and Topaz.

The young artist's lips twisted into a cynical smile. "I was just about to tell your best friend about the conversation I overheard between you and Xavier Mayne on the night of the art showing."

As Neveah watched the color leach out of Jordan's face, an awful sense of foreboding crept over her. "What conversation?"

Jordan glared at Topaz. "Get out."

He didn't budge. "I was in the men's restroom that evening when you and Mr. Mayne had your little powwow. I had the door cracked open, so I heard everything. Shame on you," he chided mockingly, shaking his head. "If you're wondering when my feelings for you changed, you need look no further than that night."

"What is he talking about, Jordan?" Neveah asked faintly, rising from the worktable on rubbery legs.

Jordan met her gaze, her eyes glazed with tears of shame and regret. "I came on to Xavier after a party at his apartment."

Neveah felt the floor tilt beneath her. "You did *what?*"

"It was thirteen years ago," Jordan hastened to rationalize.

Neveah stared at her in wounded disbelief. "How *could* you?"

"I'm sorry," Jordan whispered.

"Not sorry enough to come clean sooner," Topaz taunted.

"Get out," both women snapped at him.

He gathered up his painting and quickly departed.

Neveah and Jordan squared off across the table.

"Were you ever planning to tell me about this?" Neveah demanded.

Jordan spread her hands helplessly. "There never seemed to be a right time. The party happened in February. Four months later, you broke up with Xavier and moved to Africa!"

"And now I have to wonder if you were secretly happy about that," Neveah said bitterly.

In the second it took Jordan to drop her gaze, Neveah was struck by a horrible realization. "Oh my God," she breathed. "You're in love with him."

Jordan said nothing, but she didn't have to. The truth was written all over her guilty face.

Staggered, Neveah pressed a hand to her churning stomach. "All these years… You were always talking about falling for the wrong guy. Little did I know you were talking about *mine!*"

Tears rolled down Jordan's face. "I'm so sorry."

"You should be." Outraged, Neveah began pacing up and down the floor. "Every time you badmouthed him, every time you consoled me, every time you told me I did the right thing by leaving him, you had ulterior motives!"

"That's not true!" Jordan protested. "I saw what you went through every time he cheated on you. I saw how devastated you were that last time, when you lost the baby. I honestly *did* believe you were doing the right thing by breaking up with him!"

"Of course you did," Neveah jeered. "With me out of the picture, you were free to pursue him."

"I did no such thing!" Jordan exploded, her face contorted with sudden fury. "But even if I had, *so what?* Why do you always have to have everything? You have the perfect relationship with your mother, while my parents and I barely tolerate one another. You and I went to the same art school, but *you're* the one who had professors fawning all over you. I didn't become a famous art historian, but *you're* a world-renowned artist. Even Topaz is always raving about you! My God, Neveah, you have *everything*. Do you have to have the perfect guy, too?"

Neveah stared at Jordan as though she were seeing

a complete stranger. "So that's what this is about?" she whispered incredulously. "You were *jealous* of me?"

Jordan glowered at her. "I didn't come on to Xavier because I was trying to get back at you. I love him for the same reasons you do, and I gave in to those feelings in a moment of weakness. But that was the *only* time."

"Once was more than enough." Neveah searched her face. "Did you sleep with him that night?"

Jordan just looked at her, denying her the courtesy of a response.

"I'm outta here," Neveah muttered in disgust.

As she started from the room, Jordan burst out desperately, *"Neveah, wait!"*

When she grabbed her arm, Neveah wheeled around and slapped her across the face.

Jordan gasped sharply, clutching her reddened cheek. As fresh tears swam into her eyes, she gazed beseechingly at Neveah. "I never meant to hurt you."

"Go to hell." When Neveah reached the doorway, she paused and glanced back. "One more thing."

Jordan eyed her piteously.

"This friendship, as well as this partnership, are over." With that, Neveah turned and walked out.

Chapter 20

Her next stop was the community center.

Although the rest of the staff had gone home, Xavier was still in his office. He stood at the large picture window, his hands tucked into his pockets as he stared outside.

As Neveah strode into the room, he glanced over at her and smiled wanly. "Oh, good, you came—"

She cut him off. "Why didn't you tell me about you and Jordan?"

He looked blank. "Me and...?" As comprehension dawned, his expression turned grim. "So she finally told you."

"Not by choice. One of our artists overheard you two talking on the night of the reception. If not for him, God only knows how long you and Jordan would have kept your dirty little secret!"

Xavier frowned. "It's not what you think, Neveah. Nothing happened."

"Then why all the secrecy?" she demanded furiously. "If

nothing happened, why didn't you tell me that Jordan hit on you?"

"Because I didn't want to upset you." He gave her a pointed look.

"I don't believe you!" Neveah hissed.

He eyed her incredulously. "You actually think I slept with your best friend? While you were *right* down the hall?"

Neveah sneered. "As you recently reminded me, I used to be a featherweight when it came to holding my liquor. If memory serves, I'd had one too many drinks that night and was out cold. So you and Jordan could have been swinging from the chandelier for all I knew!"

"We weren't," Xavier snapped, advancing on her. "I turned her down, and that was the end of it. Damn it, Neveah, I can't believe we're even *having* this conversation. Didn't I already tell you I'm not attracted to Jordan?"

"You've 'told' me a lot of things over the years that weren't true," Neveah raged. "My God, Xay, she's in love with you!"

"Then she's a damn psycho," he snarled, "because I've never done *anything* to lead her on!"

"Obviously you have!" As he reached her, Neveah defiantly held her ground, hands thrust on her hips, heart hammering as she glared up at him.

"Let me tell you something, sweetheart." He got up in her face, eyes glittering with fury, heat rolling off his big body in scorching waves. Even as she wanted to lash out at him and scratch his eyes out, she found herself trembling with arousal. When she tried to turn her head away, he cupped her chin, forcing her to reckon with the blazing intensity of his gaze.

"If I wanted Jordan," he growled, "I could have had her a long time ago. You were halfway around the world while she was *right* here. I saw her around town and at different functions. I could have accepted any one of her friendly invitations to have drinks. But I never did, because God help me, you're the *only* woman I've ever wanted."

Neveah gave a harsh, cynical laugh. "Along with Alyson Kelley, and the legion of other women you've messed around with."

He flinched, the verbal missile striking home. "I've never claimed to be a monk, but one thing I *can* say is that I've never cheated on you."

Neveah froze, gaping at him incredulously. "You never cheated on me? *You never cheated on me?*"

"That's right."

"You liar!" Choking with disbelief, pain and fury, she launched herself at him, pummeling his broad chest with her fists.

After patiently enduring several blows, he captured her wrists and hauled her into his arms, pinning her against him. "Stop," he whispered hoarsely as she struggled for release. *"Please stop."*

Pushed beyond her limits, she broke down sobbing, "I can't believe you have the audacity to lie to my face!"

"I'm not lying, Neveah. I never cheated on you!"

"Damn you!" she exploded, wrenching out of his arms and retreating backward before he could recapture her. "You want to know why I left you? Because I couldn't take the madness anymore! The women, the harassing phone calls, your suspicious absences! I watched my mom go through *hell* with my father's affairs. So there was only so much I could take from you!"

Xavier shook his head at her, his jaw tightly clenched. "I wasn't unfaithful to you, Neveah. I may have done a lot of things that hurt you, but *that* wasn't one of them."

Her lips twisted contemptuously. "Do you really expect me to believe that the woman who called me from your bedroom that day was 'just a friend'?"

He frowned in confusion. "What woman?"

"The woman you met after one of the few basketball games that I missed. The woman who described your apartment to a T. The woman who shared, in explicit detail, how you'd just finished screwing her senseless."

Slowly the confusion cleared, and he swore viciously under his breath.

"Yeah." Neveah sneered. "*That* woman."

His brows slammed together over flashing dark eyes. "*That's* why you broke up with me? Because of *her?*"

"Because of many 'hers'!" Neveah shouted, glaring at him through a scalding sheen of tears. "Even as she was describing your bedroom and your sneaker collection and the cologne you wore, I was *still* willing to give you the benefit of the doubt. But then I heard your voice in the background and..." She shook her head, the pain of his betrayal just as raw as ever. "After I got off the phone with her, I was devastated. I hopped into my car and headed straight to your apartment. I was going to catch you red-handed and finally put an end to all your bullshit lies! But on my way there—"

Xavier had paled. "You got into an accident—"

"—and lost the *only* thing that would have kept us together!" she screamed.

He stared at her with an expression of shock mingled with horror. And then, to her stunned dismay, tears welled in his eyes. "You...you were *pregnant?*"

"Yes!" she shrieked, on the verge of hysteria. *"Nine weeks and three days pregnant, damn you!"*

She watched as the remaining blood drained from his face. And then she bent over, taking several deep breaths to keep from hyperventilating.

"My God." His voice was barely above a whisper. "How could you... Why didn't you *tell* me?"

"It was *your* fault!"

His face contorted.

A moment later he charged toward her, and for one awful second she feared that he might grab her and shake her, or worse. But he gathered her fiercely into his arms and held tight. When she felt his broad shoulders shaking, she realized that he was crying. If she hadn't already been sobbing, that would have undone her.

They sank weakly to their knees, holding each other, bonded by their shared sense of loss. And Neveah realized that this moment, this *connection,* was what she'd needed from him all along.

God, if only she'd realized sooner!

He kissed her forehead, rubbed his damp cheek against her hair. "I'm so sorry you went through that alone," he croaked, his voice ravaged with emotion. "I wish *to God* you'd told me. You should have."

"I know," she admitted tearfully. "I didn't know then, but I do now."

He shuddered, his arms tightening around her. She didn't know how long they knelt on the floor, silently weeping, drawing strength and healing from each other's grief. This moment had been thirteen years in the making. Right then and there, time *had* no meaning.

When they at last drew apart, they turned in unison to gaze up at the *Lavender Nymph* painting. The sweet-faced child seemed to be watching them with solemn compassion.

"Jesus." Swiping at his watery eyes, Xavier inhaled a deep, shuddering breath and gently helped Neveah to her feet. "I'm sorry, sweetheart. If I had known about our baby, there's no way I would have let you walk out of my life. I shouldn't have let you go anyway."

She smiled forlornly. "I didn't give you a choice."

"No, you didn't." His bright eyes tunneled into hers. "You need to know what really happened that day."

She shook her head. "It's not—"

"No, it *is* important! You tried and convicted me without giving me a chance to defend myself. So let me set the record straight once and for all. I *did* meet that woman after a game. I don't even remember her name, that's how insignificant she was. I didn't hook up with her. She'd seen you at the games before, so she knew you were my girlfriend. One of my teammates must have given her my address, 'cause she showed up unexpectedly that day, claiming she was visiting a friend in the building who wasn't home. I told her I had somewhere to go, so she left. But she came right back and said her car needed a jump, so I went downstairs with her. But her battery was fine. While I was under the hood trying to figure out the problem, she asked if she could use my bathroom. I had *no* idea she'd go through my address book and call you with that bullshit story."

Neveah reached up, rubbing her forehead with trembling fingers. And just like that, she knew he was telling the truth. She wanted to curl up in a ball and weep for all the years she'd foolishly wasted.

Her voice quavered as she said, "Put yourself in my shoes—"

"I have," Xavier interrupted. "And I can tell you that if it had been *me,* I would have given you a chance to explain yourself. Don't you think you owed me that much?" He shook his head in wounded disbelief. "But that's not even the worst part of it. The fact that you thought so little of me, of *us,* that you would believe I was capable of betraying you that way—that's the worst part."

Guilt swept through her. "Xay, we'd dealt with the cheating issues before—"

"All the more reason for you to confront me and ask what was up! You meant the world to me, Neveah. If you don't know that by now, then—" He cut himself short, swearing under his breath as he glanced away from her.

"Xay, please understand where I was coming from. We'd been having so many problems. You're not blameless here, as you've acknowledged yourself."

His jaw hardened for one prolonged moment. Then, just as swiftly as the anger had ignited, it was gone, like a storm passing over the horizon. The expression that came over his face was bleak, full of disillusionment.

"I don't even think you understand how terrified I was when I saw you lying in that hospital bed," he said without inflection. "When your mom called to tell me you'd been in an accident, I must have died a thousand deaths. And I was absolutely devastated when you told me we'd grown apart. I knew I'd hurt and disappointed you, but I never would have imagined that you'd leave the country without saying goodbye or telling me where you were going. You even swore your mom and friends to secrecy." He shook his head at her. "I guess I took for granted that we'd always be together, that we'd get through our problems because our love was strong enough to survive anything. But maybe I was wrong. Even after the recent breakthrough we've had, you still thought I'd slept with Jordan."

Neveah could sense him retreating from her, but she didn't know how to stop it from happening. "Why have you been acting so distant lately?" she cried out. "For the past three days, you've treated me like a stranger! And then I see Alyson Kelley sashaying out of your office like—"

Xavier sighed. "For the last time, there's nothing going on between me and Alyson. When I ran into her at the reception that night, she said she was looking for a job and would love to work at the community center. I promised her an interview, but when she showed up dressed to seduce, I knew there was no way I could ever hire her. As for my mood this week, you're right, I haven't been myself. I'm sorry for not confiding in you sooner, but I've been trying to sort through some things."

"What things?"

He hesitated. "My father's back."

Neveah gasped, her eyes widening in shock. "Your *father?*"

He nodded grimly. "He showed up at my house one night while you were out of town. I haven't even told my family. I didn't want to upset them."

"What did he want?"

"He's practically homeless. He got himself clean for a while, then fell on hard times and started using again. He's been going through serious withdrawal over the past three days."

"And you've been taking care of him," Neveah surmised, awed by the depth of his compassion for the man who'd nearly destroyed him. "You haven't been out of the office attending meetings. You've been going home to look after him."

"Not by myself. I've hired two nurses who specialize in addiction treatment. Once he's a little stronger, I'm placing him in a private rehab center." Xavier glanced at his watch. "Which reminds me, I have an appointment to tour the facility tonight, so I should be going soon."

"Do you want me to go with you?" Neveah offered.

"No."

She flinched, stung by his refusal.

He reached out, gently cupping her cheek. "I love you. No matter what happens between us, that won't ever change. But you've given me a lot to think about tonight."

She swallowed with difficulty. There was so much more she could tell him, so much she should say, but it was too late. She saw it in his remote eyes, and it tore her apart.

As he walked to his desk and sat down, she murmured,

"Yasmin told me you're leaving tomorrow to be the keynote speaker at a leadership conference in Boston."

He nodded.

"Congratulations. And…have a good trip."

"Thanks." He was no longer looking at her.

So for the second time that day, Neveah turned and walked out on one of the most important relationships she'd ever had in her life.

But this time, it wasn't on her terms.

Chapter 21

Neveah was awakened by the gentle stroke of a hand across her cheek. Opening her eyes, she saw her mother smiling quietly at her.

Raising her head from the starched white sheet that covered the hospital bed, Neveah kissed Delores's hand and held it against her face. "You're awake."

"Have been for a while. I was just watching you sleep, something I've missed doing."

Neveah smiled at her. "The doctor says your surgery was a complete success, Mama. They performed the hysterectomy and you're cancer-free."

"I know. He told me." Delores sighed. "God is good."

"Amen," Neveah fervently agreed.

Delores squeezed her hand. "He also said you've been a trouper all day. Although you *were* starting to drive the nurses crazy, demanding updates every hour."

Neveah grinned sheepishly. "It would have been every *half* hour if Randall and Xavier hadn't intervened."

Delores chuckled. "I'm glad they were both here to restrain you."

"Me, too."

Neveah had been surprised, and overcome with gratitude, when Xavier showed up at the hospital that afternoon, arriving straight from the airport. Although she still didn't know the fate of their relationship, she'd thoroughly appreciated having his shoulder to lean on.

She grinned at her mother, holding a cup of water to her mouth. "Randall says he's taking you on another trip, but he kept the destination a secret to give you an added incentive to pull through the surgery. Sounds like you two are getting pretty serious."

"Let's just say we're taking things one day at a time," Delores said enigmatically.

"Uh-huh. Well, don't do anything crazy like eloping during your next rendezvous. As you always used to tell me, I don't want to be deprived of crying at your wedding."

"Yes, ma'am." Delores smiled, searching her daughter's face. "Speaking of weddings, I hope to start planning yours once I'm back on my feet."

Sobering, Neveah ducked her head. "I don't think I have any broom-hopping plans in my immediate future, Mama. I didn't want to tell you before the surgery, but Xavier and I are on hiatus…indefinitely."

"You didn't have to tell me," Delores said gently. "I can always sense when something's wrong with you, and I knew it went much deeper than your quarrel with Jordan."

Neveah met her mother's gaze. "Do you remember that Wolof proverb you once told me? The one you never translated?"

Delores nodded. "'A woman's heart can be as transparent as the nose on her face.'"

Neveah stared at her. "So you've always known how Jordan felt about Xavier?"

"I suspected. It was the way she looked at him, hung on to his every word."

"How did *I* not see that?" Neveah muttered.

"Maybe you didn't want to," Delores said quietly. "Anyway, I knew how much her friendship meant to you, so I didn't want to hurt you by sharing my suspicions. I'm sure that's why Xavier held his tongue, too."

Neveah nodded slowly, wishing she'd never accused him of sleeping with Jordan. Yet another regret that would plague her for years.

Shaking off the dismal thought, she glanced at her watch. "Visiting hours are almost over. Let me get Randall so he can spend more time with you."

"No need," Delores said. "He and Xavier had to leave to visit someone, so they came by to say good-night while you were napping."

Neveah's mind flashed on an earlier image of Randall and Xavier huddled in a corner, deep in conversation. When Randall pulled his nephew into a tight hug, she'd concluded that Xavier must have told him about his father's return.

"As for you and Xavier," Delores continued, "I wouldn't be too sure about that hiatus. I saw the way he was looking at you before he and Randall left. You didn't even wake up when he kissed your cheek."

"He did?"

"Yep. And now I have a confession to make." Delores's gaze softened. "I'm the one who told Xavier you were coming back home."

Stunned, Neveah gaped at her. "*You* told him? Why?"

Tears misted her mother's eyes. "In case I didn't make it, I wanted to leave this earth knowing that you and Xavier were together…where you belong."

Chapter 22

Three weeks later

The crowd was buzzing with anticipation. Reporters, politicians and members of the community had gathered for the public unveiling of the mural. Once all the speeches had been made, Xavier returned to the podium to formally introduce Neveah.

"When I decided to commission an artist to paint the mural," he began, "there was only one person I wanted for the job, and anyone who's ever seen Neveah Symon's work knows why. Unfortunately, she'd been living overseas for the past several years, so I wasn't exactly sure how I was going to get the mural done. And then fate intervened—" he met Neveah's gaze "—and suddenly, there she was…home. Now, I haven't seen the mural yet, so right now I'm feeling as excited as, well, a groom waiting to lift his bride's veil."

Neveah stared at him as a wave of appreciative sighs and whispers swept around the large hall.

"So without further ado," he announced, turning to the curtained wall behind him, "let's lift the veil."

As the mural was revealed, the audience erupted into thunderous applause that both delighted and humbled Neveah. But it was Xavier's awestruck expression that brought tears to her eyes. She'd been nervously anticipating his reaction to the finished work—a vibrant, multilayered mosaic of familiar faces, themes and images that represented the proud community.

When he turned and beckoned to Neveah to join him at the podium, her mother, Yasmin, Yolanda and Raina practically pushed her out of her chair. The crowd showered her with cheers and whistles as she walked to the podium, where Xavier assisted her onto the platform and leaned close to murmur, "It's absolutely perfect. *Thank you.*"

"Thank *you*," she whispered to him.

"Speech!" someone called out, which was followed by enthusiastic echoes of agreement.

Xavier smiled at Neveah. "Go on. Say something."

Trembling with nerves, she turned to the podium and began shyly, "I'm not much of an orator. I've always been more comfortable with a paintbrush than a microphone. But since you folks have been so kind, I'd like to share some of the inspiration behind the mural. The title, *Imagine Us,* was actually inspired by something Xavier told me not too long ago."

Catching the wicked gleam in his eyes, she blushed and cleared her throat before continuing. "I grew up in the Third Ward, and although I've been away for a while, I've never forgotten where I came from. Since returning home, I've learned about the healing power of forgiveness, and I've watched people I love overcome impossible challenges. While attending last month's Labor Day picnic, I was awed by the spirit of unity, hope and resilience I saw in each of you. This mural is dedicated to every member of the community—young and old—who has ever dared to dream against all odds. *Imagine Us* is an homage to second chances, the miracle of love and redemption and the unshakable belief that *anything* is possible."

As the audience reacted with deafening applause, Xavier gazed wonderingly at Neveah. "I thought you weren't an orator."

Too choked up to respond, she merely shrugged and smiled.

"Talk about a tough act to follow," Xavier said, addressing the audience. "I don't think there's a dry eye in the house. Even my mama's crying."

Neveah looked, and sure enough, Birdie was dabbing at the corners of her eyes. Meeting Neveah's stunned gaze, she gave a subtle nod that conveyed more than any words could have.

"Not to upstage that amazing speech," Xavier continued, staring at Neveah, "but there's something I've been wanting to ask that's long overdue."

Neveah watched, heart pounding, as he sank to one knee, drawing a collective gasp from the spectators.

Gazing deep into her eyes, he said huskily, "I love you, Neveah. I can't live another day without you. So will you put me out of my misery and marry me?"

"Oh my God." As tears rushed to her eyes, Neveah looked to the riveted crowd. "What do you say, ladies? Can I take another Mayne off the market?"

Her query was met by a hearty swell of laughter mingled with feminine groans. "We'll forgive you!" one woman assented.

"In that case." Choking with sobs of joy and laughter, Neveah threw her arms around Xavier's neck and cried, *"Yes, I'll marry you!"*

He stood and crushed his mouth to hers, then swept her into his arms and spun her around as a roar of cheers erupted around the hall. As their lips reluctantly parted, Xavier removed a small jewelry box from his breast pocket and told the celebrating crowd, "If you folks would excuse us for a minute, we need to, ah, make sure the ring fits."

As he carried her from the hall amid chanting and applause, Neveah smiled up at him. "Is this going to become a habit of yours?"

He grinned wickedly. "Sweetheart, you ain't seen *nothing* yet."

The ring fit, of course. Xavier knew every exquisite inch of Neveah's body, which he demonstrated to her later that evening. Over and over again, until she breathlessly begged for mercy.

Afterward, they wound up on the porch swing cuddling beneath a large, downy blanket as they listened to the gently falling rain. The rain seemed to represent a cleansing of their stormy past. A new beginning.

Tenderly caressing her face, Xavier murmured, "Mama's already planning our engagement party and wedding."

Neveah chuckled, her arms looped around his neck as she sat astride him. "That must be what she and my mom were discussing during the reception earlier. Between those two, I don't think we're going to have much input in our own wedding."

Xavier grinned. "That's probably a safe assumption. But, honestly, I don't care where we get married or what kind of flowers we have. All that matters, sweetheart, is that we do the damn thing. And the sooner, the better."

Neveah smiled. "I couldn't agree more."

He winked. "Then you're already off to a good start, wife."

She laughed, and the sound was pure music to his ears.

As addictive as her sweet, familiar scent. The lushness of her thighs straddling his. The radiant beauty of her face.

"I want to teach an art class at the community center," she said.

"Really?"

She nodded. "I was blessed with instructors who nurtured my love for art. I'd like to do the same for others."

His chest swelled with pride and gratitude. "That'd be wonderful, sweetheart. Everyone's gonna be so excited."

"Me, too." She nibbled his lower lip, smiling into his eyes. "I love you so much, Xay. I never stopped."

"Thank God." Xavier didn't think he could possibly be any happier than he was at that moment.

But he was wrong.

"Maybe it *would* be best if we let our mamas handle the wedding plans," Neveah said with a sigh. "Between painting, teaching, lovemaking and nesting, I honestly don't know how much energy I'll have left."

Xavier went still, searching her face in the rain-silvered moonlight. "Did you just say you'll be...*nesting?*"

Holding his gaze, Neveah took his hand and gently placed it over her flat stomach. "About ten weeks from now, you're going to feel your child moving inside me."

Stunned, Xavier stared at her. "You're...pregnant?"

She grinned. "Um, yeah."

Bursting with euphoria, he lunged to his feet and swung her around as her rapturous peal of laughter rang out. Suddenly fearing that he'd make her dizzy, or somehow hurt their child, he stopped and gingerly returned to the swing.

"When did it happen?" he whispered, gazing into her face. "When did you find out?"

"It must have happened the day after the charity auction. That was the first time we'd made love without protection." She smiled. "I've been so tired lately, but I was afraid to hope that I might be pregnant. But Mama started speculating, so I agreed to make a doctor's appointment. I just got the results this morning. If you hadn't beaten me to it, *I* would have proposed to *you*."

Xavier laughed. "A baby," he marveled, lovingly stroking her cheek. "We're going to have a *baby*."

She nodded, her eyes shimmering with tears that reflected his own. "We're getting our lavender nymph."

As Xavier's heart soared even higher, he caught her face between his hands and kissed her, unleashing a lifetime of love, adoration, passion and devotion. By the time he drew away, Neveah was breathless and trembling.

"I'm gonna be so good to you," he vowed fiercely. "I'm gonna take care of you, and make you so damn happy."

She smiled tenderly. "You already have."

He kissed her again, then gently curved his hand against her belly, awed by the thought of a tiny life growing inside her. A life they'd created together.

"Do you need anything?"

"You," Neveah whispered. "I only need *you*."

To demonstrate, she parted their robes and provocatively rubbed herself against him, crooning when he grew instantly hard.

"Are you sure you're up for another round?" he asked, cupping her bottom.

A naughty gleam filled her eyes. "With all these raging hormones in my system," she purred, lowering onto his erection, "I'll be *up* for a while."

"Lucky me," Xavier murmured, thrusting deep inside her.

He'd gotten his fairy-tale ending, and then some.

* * * * *

NATIONAL BESTSELLING AUTHOR

ROCHELLE ALERS

Actress Regina Cole stunned the world when she gave up her career to marry an older man. After his death, Regina encounters his estranged son, Dr. Aaron Spencer, and is unable to deny the instant attraction. Suddenly Aaron's quest for revenge pales in comparison to his desire for Regina....

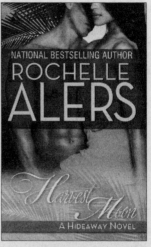

HARVEST MOON
A HIDEAWAY NOVEL

"Alers has written a sensual, spellbinding romance that upholds the most excellent tradition of classic romance literature."
—*RT Book Reviews* on *HARVEST MOON*

KIMANI PRESS™

Coming the first week of May 2011 wherever books are sold.

www.kimanipress.com

KPRA4440511

*She's casting her
ballot—for love*

KIMANI ROMANCE

Essence
bestselling author
DONNA
HILL

SECRET
Attraction

SECRET
Attraction

DONNA
HILL

ESSENCE BESTSELLING AUTHOR

LAWSONS *of* LOUISIANA

Heiress to a political dynasty, Desiree Lawson is more interested
in tossing her hat in the ring than playing the field. But when she
is fixed up with Spence Hampton, she has a change of heart. Can
the charismatic playboy convince Desiree that his bachelor days
are over—and become the top candidate for her heart?

"If you miss this book, you'll miss something special and
wonderful: a potentially enriching experience."
—*RT Book Reviews* on *A PRIVATE AFFAIR*

*Coming the first week of May 2011
wherever books are sold.*

KIMANI
ROMANCE

www.kimanipress.com

KPDH2080511

They're answering
the passionate call
of the Wilde....

KIMANI ROMANCE

To Desire a

WILDE

Favorite author
*Kimberly Kaye
Terry*

To Desire a WILDE

Wilde IN WYOMING

Kimberly Kaye Terry

Shilah Wilde's home, Wilde Ranch, is always where his heart
is. So when its future is threatened, he's the first to defend the
sprawling Western spread—even if it means going head-to-
head against veterinarian Ellie Crandall. The shy girl he once
knew has matured into a stunning, sensual beauty...and it
will be his pleasure to rein her in!

Wilde IN **WYOMING** *Saddle Up...to a Wilde*

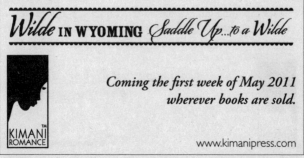

*Coming the first week of May 2011
wherever books are sold.*

KIMANI™
ROMANCE

www.kimanipress.com

KPKKT2090511

They're getting
up close…
and personal.

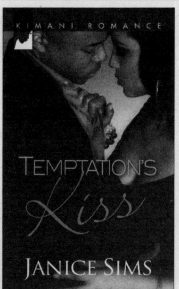

TEMPTATION'S
Kiss

JANICE
SIMS

Patrice Sutton has just snagged the female lead opposite
devastatingly handsome movie idol T. K. McKenna. And
the burgeoning film star is showing T.K. a passion more real
than anything he's ever experienced on-screen. But what
will it take to prove to her that she's the only woman he'll
ever desire—and love—off the set?

"Compelling characters…a terrific setting and great
secondary characters showcase Sims's talent for penning
great stories."—*RT Book Reviews* on *Temptation's Song*

*Coming the first week of May 2011
wherever books are sold.*

www.kimanipress.com

KPJS2100511